"Ah, all right. Well, if the time comes and you wanna talk about it, feel free to come to me, all right?"

With that, Rika walked past Emeralda and away from the building. As she watched her go, Emeralda smiled a little.

"I think I understand a little why Emilia cherishes your friendship so much..."

But even that light smile quickly sank into the darkness.

"Well, I must be going..."

She rose to her feet, then up in the air, taking flight as she made a beeline for the Sasaki residence.

"Satan...the Devil King, Satan..."

The malice was palpable in the words spilling from her lips.

"I swear I'll make you pay."

The Devil Is Interviewed

"So, Marko, how long have you been a demon anyway?"

"Did you have any strong reason for selecting your current appearance and living situation?"

It was structured more like an interview than a proper interrogation.

"How did you learn the Japanese language? And you speak English, too, right?"

"What's the hardest part of learning a language you don't know at all?"

To the casual observer, a man seated at a desk facing two managers wouldn't look like anything more or less than a run-of-the-mill job interview.

"What did you put the most effort into in your life before you began working at the Hatagaya Station MgRonald?"

"Now that you've established relationships with the people around you, what are your goals for the future?"

"Um, c-can you guys calm down a little bit?"

Maou, his identity as the Devil King of another world now revealed, was being raked over the coals by Mayumi Kisaki and Kotomi Iwaki, his former and current bosses at MgRonald. Thanks to Chiho's out-of-control behavior, most of the main staff at this MgRonald now knew his secret. Maou didn't blame her for that, but he certainly didn't expect this managerial intervention afterward.

"Um, I-I know I'm not really in a position to say this...but aren't there other things you're concerned about?"

Yes, his secret was out. But between Chiho and Suzuno's mind-boggling behavior and hurried explanations—to say nothing of Acieth's incomprehensible appetite—he figured there was plenty that should

The Devil King of an alien world bowed his head to them. The two MgRonald full-timers chuckled in response.

"Right now, there's just one thing I need from you: Keep working hard like you always do to help out Ms. Iwaki."

"There's some kind of big battle coming up, right? I know everyone on our part-time roll has their own life to live, and it's not my job to pry into them, but please don't get yourself killed or anything, all right? Because there's absolutely no way I'll be able to find someone to fill your shifts."

Maou kept his head low, almost burrowing into the floor with it.

"...I've pretty much been a demon ever since the day I was born. My appearance now just happened naturally. It's possible for me to change back, but not for very long, so my first priority was finding ample food and shelter. Right now, my main goal is to maintain my life in Japan without having anyone talking behind my back..."

With that, he began answering their interview questions as best he could without holding anything back.

The Devil Is Hated

"...Emeralda? What are you doing here with something like that?"

Rika Suzuki couldn't help but ask the question after she found Emeralda sitting on the outer walkway of Villa Rosa Sasazuka. Emeralda looked up at her, a bit quizzical.

"Why do you seem so concerned? This is just a smaaall bit of gold."

"There's no way that's anything normal..."

"Now it's my turn to ask a question. Why were you coming down from upstairs, Rika, hmm? From the Devil King's apartment, no less?"

"I just got back from Ente Isla. Ashiya and Urushihara asked me to take care of some things, so lately I've been visiting Devil's Castle, as long as the lizard's not acting up. More importantly, is that thing real?"

In Emeralda's hand was a rectangular, golden object the size of a smartphone.

"It's puuure gold, certified grade A by Saint Aile. Can I sell this in Japan, do you think?"

"Please don't. It'll raise way too many questions and be a massive pain."

"Awww, will it? But Emilia said she got some coins changed a whiiile back."

"Well, coins are one thing, but a whole bar is worth millions of yen! What are you even trying to buy with it anyway?!"

"Hmm, weeell, I'd probably start with some classic Sentucky Fried Chicken." Rika tilted her head back, exasperated. "You could buy your own industrial chicken farm with that much."

"Is that a bad thing?"

"If you bring that much gold to a pawn shop, they're definitely going to ask you where you got it, is all. That and there are probably going to be tax problems. I don't think you'll be able to find someplace that'll buy it."

"Reeeally? Hmm, how about this, then?"

The disappointed woman put the bar back in her pocket, despite Rika's concerns about its weight possibly tearing her blouse, then took out a small bag and showed it to her friend. Looking inside, Rika found what appeared to be dried nuts or berries, except they resembled and smelled like nothing she'd ever seen before.

"...Are these spices, or some kind of special tea or something?"

"Oooh, good eye. That's correct. This is more of the best that Saint Aile has to offer."

"...Couldn't you have just brought along some coins or jewels or whatever?"

Jewelry would be much easier to pawn off, at least. Unfortunately, Rika didn't know any place on Earth capable of appraising the agricultural produce of another planet.

"...How about I just lend you some money?" Rika took a ten-thousand-yen note out from her wallet and offered it to Emeralda.

"Oooh! Thank you sooo much! You can keep these Gidet nuts in exchange. I'll pay you back later, okaaay?"

She handed the bag of nuts to Rika.

"If you boil these, grind them into a powder, warm it up, and sprinkle it on some bread, it's veeery tasty and refreshing."

"The name, the preparation, the taste... It's all a mystery to me, Emeralda."

Rika scratched her head a bit, then looked up at the building's second-floor walkway. "What brought you here instead of Emi's place anyway?"

"I just had a liiitle business with the Devil King, and I was hoping to catch him alone..."

"Oh? Maou? What's up with him?"

"You didn't hear the news?"

"No, what?"

Surprisingly, Rika didn't seem to notice when the drawl disappeared from Emeralda's voice.

"I think Emi will tell you about it...in time."

"Hmm... Well, are you still going to SFC? If you're about to have lunch, I can come with."

"...Apologies. I was actually planning to visit Chiho's house next."

Emeralda stood up, her voice soft but resolute. Only then did Rika pick up on Emeralda's resolve. She decided to not press the matter any further.

take priority. At his question, the managers simply glanced at each other before quickly answering.

"No."

"Not really."

Kisaki and Iwaki did seem a little flustered, though.

"I mean, I still haven't gotten over the shock, and I'm not completely convinced, either."

"At the same time, there's not a lot we can do about this anyway. Or ask you about."

"You've been working here a long time now. There are no issues with your status or documentation or whatnot. And if we fired you because you're a demon, you wouldn't find that very fair, would you?"

"In fact, I'd be kind of scared to."

"Oh, n-no, um...yeah."

This was all far beyond anything Maou expected. He didn't know why it all felt so strange but something was definitely not right.

"But now that we know this...well, we're all grown-ups here. I'd like to build a baseline of knowledge to work with. That's what this interview is for."

"Right. After all, if there winds up being some big problem because you're a Devil King and Yusa is a Hero and so on, the blame's going to fall on Ms. Kisaki for hiring you and me for my part in managing you... Oh, but no offense meant by that! Again, this is just research on our part!"

Iwaki's awkward attempt to keep things cordial made Kisaki visibly wince. That surprised Maou. It was an unexpectedly emotional moment for him. At its core, his identity as the Devil King and Emi's duty to oppose him as the Hero were the real reasons why Acieth had fired off laser beams and damaged the MgRonald dining area in a bout of hunger. But neither Kisaki nor Iwaki seemed to think that way. They were simply concerned about Sadao Maou and Emi Yusa.

"...I'm really sorry for causing you guys so much trouble."

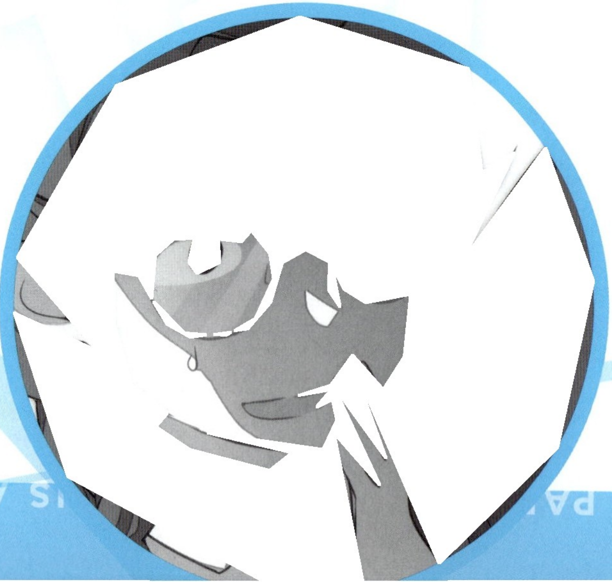

SATOSHI WAGAHARA
ILLUSTRATED BY 029 (ONIKU)

NEW YORK

THE DEVIL IS A PART-TIMER!, Volume 20
SATOSHI WAGAHARA, ILLUSTRATION BY 029 (ONIKU)

Translation by Kevin Gifford
Cover art by 029 (oniku)

This book is a work of fiction. Names, characters, places, and incidents are the product of the author's imagination or are used fictitiously. Any resemblance to actual events, locales, or persons, living or dead, is coincidental.

HATARAKU MAOUSAMA!, Volume 20
© Satoshi Wagahara 2018
Edited by Dengeki Bunko
First published in Japan in 2018 by KADOKAWA CORPORATION, Tokyo.
English translation rights arranged with KADOKAWA CORPORATION, Tokyo, through Tuttle-Mori Agency, Inc., Tokyo.

English translation © 2021 by Yen Press, LLC

Yen Press, LLC supports the right to free expression and the value of copyright. The purpose of copyright is to encourage writers and artists to produce the creative works that enrich our culture.

The scanning, uploading, and distribution of this book without permission is a theft of the author's intellectual property. If you would like permission to use material from the book (other than for review purposes), please contact the publisher. Thank you for your support of the author's rights.

Yen On
150 West 30th Street, 19th Floor
New York, NY 10001

Visit us at yenpress.com
facebook.com/yenpress
twitter.com/yenpress
yenpress.tumblr.com
instagram.com/yenpress

First Yen On Edition: August 2021

Yen On is an imprint of Yen Press, LLC.
The Yen On name and logo are trademarks of Yen Press, LLC.

The publisher is not responsible for websites (or their content) that are not owned by the publisher.

Library of Congress Cataloging-in-Publication Data
Names: Wagahara, Satoshi. | 029 (Light novel illustrator) illustrator. | Gifford, Kevin, translator. | Steinbach, Kevin, translator.
Title: The devil is a part-timer! / Satoshi Wagahara ; translation by Kevin Gifford ; illustration by 029 (oniku) ; translation by Kevin Steinbach.
Other titles: Hataraku Maousama!. English
Description: First Yen On edition. | New York, NY : Yen On, 2015–
Identifiers: LCCN 2015028390 |
ISBN 9780316383127 (v. 1 : pbk.) |
ISBN 9780316385015 (v. 2 : pbk.) |
ISBN 9780316385022 (v. 3 : pbk.) |
ISBN 9780316385039 (v. 4 : pbk.) |
ISBN 9780316385046 (v. 5 : pbk.) |
ISBN 9780316385060 (v. 6 : pbk.) |
ISBN 9780316469364 (v. 7 : pbk.) |
ISBN 9780316473910 (v. 8 : pbk.) |
ISBN 9780316474184 (v. 9 : pbk.) |
ISBN 9780316474207 (v. 10 : pbk.) |
ISBN 9780316474238 (v. 11 : pbk.) |
ISBN 9780316474252 (v. 12 : pbk.) |
ISBN 9780316302658 (v. 13 : pbk.) |
ISBN 9781975302672 (v. 14 : pbk.) |
ISBN 9781975302696 (v. 15 : pbk.) |
ISBN 9781975302719 (v. 16 : pbk.) |
ISBN 9781975302733 (v. 17 : pbk.) |
ISBN 9781975316327 (v. 18 : pbk.) |
ISBN 9781975316341 (v. 19 : pbk.) |
ISBN 9781975316365 (v. 20 : pbk.)
Subjects: CYAC: Fantasy.
Classification: LCC PZ7.W34 Ha 2015 | DDC [Fic]—dc23
LC record available at http://lccn.loc.gov/2015028390

ISBNs: 978-1-9753-1636-5 (paperback)
978-1-9753-1637-2 (ebook)

1 3 5 7 9 10 8 6 4 2

LSC-C

Printed in the United States of America

Devil's Castle was under siege by an archangel.

"Ma—*ohhhhhhhhhhhhhhh!!!*"

"Daahh?!"

At the front door to Room 201 of Villa Rosa Sasazuka was Mitsuki Sarue, aka the archangel Sariel—lips shaking and voice hoarse as he squared up as best he could with his tiny frame.

"Don't pretend you don't know why I dragged myself all the way oooover heeeere!!"

In what world would Maou understand why a man who was in many ways his business rival was visiting him this early on a weekday?

"Umm...did you get caught in some blowback?" Maou asked. It was actually pretty easy for him to picture it.

"What have you...you *people*...been doing?" Sariel had presented a forceful front, but now he was clinging to Maou like a newborn fawn, various emotions raging like a storm within his eyes. "What did you all *say* to Ms. Kisaki?!"

"Ahh," Maou began, playing the fool, "yeah, she stopped by the restaurant for the first time in a while. Nothing really major happened, though..."

Sariel blew spittle out the corners of his mouth. "She called me, and the first thing she said was 'Is your real name Sariel?'!!"

"………Oh." Maou resigned himself to his fate. "Sorry. Actually, a bunch of stuff happened."

"Could you try to sound serious about this?!"

"Well, um, listen, I'm just gonna tell you the truth, okay?"

"What is it?!"

"I completely forgot about you. Things were kind of, y'know, hurried."

"Seriously?!"

"What do you expect?! I didn't think I'd have my cover blown in front of everyone like that, either! And things are hard for us right now, too!"

"Well, now it's pretty goddamn clear you're not managerial material! Because if someone's lodging a complaint against you, the one thing you *don't* want to say is 'Oh, wah, wah, it's hard for me, too!'"

"Why are you even here?! If you're here to whine, the only thing I have to apologize for is not telling you sooner! As for everything getting revealed…" Maou paused for a second. But he decided to press on without much more thought. This was Sariel, after all. "This isn't my fault at all!"

"You liar! Even if *you* didn't reveal it, it's still indirectly your fault!"

"How so?!"

"Ms. Kisaki told me! She said Chiho Sasaki gave her the full rundown!"

"Yeah, and?"

"I don't know exactly why, but Chiho Sasaki's a Great Demon General on Earth, isn't she? She answers directly to you! If you're a Devil King, then control your damn officer corps!"

The term "Great Demon General" made Maou flinch a bit. "Look," he countered, "all my Demon Generals, Ashiya included, are people who were after my life at one point or another in the past. They're not gonna fall into line just because I tell them to."

"They're all loose cannons! Literally!"

Sariel stamped his foot. But not even Maou could do much about it. He couldn't change the truth at this point. If he wanted to take what Sariel now called "Chiho's sinister plot" and erase it from existence, it'd have to involve messing with the memories of many people—a measure the demons always had filed in the backs of their minds, but never did actually go through with.

"What... What am I supposed to do now...?"

Still, witnessing Sariel in the depths of despair, even Maou couldn't help but feel slightly guilty about it all.

※

Sadao Maou, doing business as Satan the Devil King elsewhere, was on the staff at the MgRonald in front of Hatagaya Station, a fast-food joint full of people who had changed his outlook on life and humanity. His former boss, Mayumi Kisaki, in particular, was his ideal in human society, a goal for him to strive for—as a non-demon anyway. However, Mayumi Kisaki, despite raising Maou up to a potential managerial candidate at lightning speed and even recommending him for a full-time training stint, had no idea about who he really was.

Until last week, that is. It all started when Acieth Alla fell ill. She was always a remarkably big eater, but one day, it began to get truly out of hand—such that, if she felt even the slightest bit hungry, she started firing beams from her face that wrecked her surroundings.

Nearly everyone Maou knew over at Villa Rosa Sasazuka pitched in to cook for her, but even that wasn't enough. So, out of desperation, Chiho Sasaki—the first person in Japan to learn about Maou and Ente Isla—took her to the Hatagaya MgRonald, where he worked. Maou still didn't really understand why she did that or how she was even able to arrange for it. Amane Ohguro—the niece of Miki Shiba, the Earth Sephirah descendant and landlord at Maou's place—was clearly involved, but Maou had no way of ascertaining how. He wanted to ask Suzuno, who was at Chiho's side the whole time assisting her...but she had left for Ente Isla the day after, a busy woman.

In normal times, Suzuno definitely would have stepped up to stop Chiho before she went on a rampage like that. But even Suzuno had been acting bizarre lately. The day before Chiho took the out-of-control Acieth to MgRonald, Suzuno told him something completely out of the blue. Suzuno Kamazuki, a woman once feared as the "Scythe of Death," a woman prudent of mind and experienced in life, had confessed her love for Maou—to *Maou*, of all people.

Until that point, Maou thought the phrase "I went completely blank" was just a metaphor, but now that he had experienced it for himself, that was the only way he found to define that instant. His vision constricted, his heart and stomach plummeting downward. He could tell Suzuno meant what she said; they had known each other long enough for that. That was why it threw Maou into so much confusion—and, blinded by the fallout, he ran away.

Now he wondered whether that connected to Chiho's out-of-line behavior at all—but the die had been cast. Taking Acieth and her impossible-to-explain affliction to MgRonald revealed just what Chiho was involved with to ex-boss Mayumi Kisaki, current manager Kotomi Iwaki, and fellow kitchen staff Takefumi Kawata and Akiko Ohki. The whole bit was out—who Maou, Emi, Alas Ramus, Acieth, and even Libicocco were, and where they came from.

At the time Maou and Emi were too dazed to handle this sea change adeptly. Simply keeping everyone calm kept their hands full.

But something didn't quite dawn on them that day.

Something that was the fact that revealing everything affected more than just Maou and Emi. Now Sariel was involved in the mix—and it was a week later when he beat down Maou's door for an explanation.

✳

"...Honestly, Emi and I don't know what to do about it, and I'm pretty sure it's even worse for Ms. Kisaki, and Ms. Iwaki and Kawacchi and Aki...um, I mean Kawata and Ohki. I think they're pretty scared, frankly. And thanks to the place getting wrecked, we had to close for three days straight, and in the midst of it all, I forgot to mention that I talked about you, too, so…sorry."

Maou was trying to be at least a little sincere with his apology. His words must have beat against Sariel's brain, as he was finally on his knees after a near-eternity of whining and howling. After a bit, Sariel said, "No. It's fine."

"Huh?"

"I don't resent you for this."

"Didn't you just say you were complaining to me?"

"Well, yes, I am. But this also means that I no longer need to deceive Ms. Kisaki about who I am."

"You were hiding more than your name before now?" Maou couldn't help but ask. In his eyes, Sariel hadn't kept much of anything from her besides his real name. Everything else was laid out in pretty honest detail in that explosive moment they first met.

"But was there anything else? I mean, if this led to, like, you and Ms. Kisaki calling off your plans to go independent, then I'd feel a little sorrier about it, but…," Maou said, despite not looking that sorry.

Sariel shook his head at Maou. "That is what I feared the most. Instead, Ms. Kisaki asked me if I've ever used magic as a cheat in my business career. That's all! I suppose she was talking about sorcery or holy energy or the like, right? So I swore to all the gods of heaven and earth that I haven't."

"Wouldn't you kind of *be* one of those gods? But…yes, I'm sorry I didn't get around to telling you. Like I said, it's not just Ms. Kisaki, but Ms. Iwaki, Kawata, and Ohki who all know, so if you could learn to recognize their names and faces, that'll be really helpful. Anyway, I gotta go in for a shift…"

"Whoa, we're not done yet."

"What? So they found out. What's the big deal?"

"No! I—I just need to check on something!"

"What more do you need…?"

"You didn't say anything *besides* my identity, did you?!"

"Hmm?"

"They know I'm from another world, that I'm an angel and not human, and that I have sorcery. They don't know anything else?!"

Despite the momentum that first brought him here, there was a twinge of terror to Sariel's voice now. Maou thought over the question for a moment. Then something came to him.

"Well, it's Acieth's fault that the cat got out of the bag, you know. So I had to tell them that you angels and your world are me and Emi's foes right now."

"I don't care about anything *that* big!"

"Look," Maou said as he dragged Sariel out the door with him, locking it up before leisurely going down the stairs, "don't worry. I didn't say anything about you kidnapping Chi and Emi, then trying to rip Emi's clothes off her. *Yet*."

Sariel clutched his head and scream. "*Nooooooooooooooooooo!!!!*"

"And *that's* what they call bringing trouble upon yourself," Maou finished.

To Sariel, who had mastered life in Japan much faster than Maou and Ashiya, and who had made no effort to hide his infatuation with Mayumi Kisaki, the things he'd done during the demon war were a dark blemish never to be revealed. Maou, to his credit, had no interest in engineering Sariel's downfall. After all, despite the groaning he could still hear from upstairs, Sariel was just as good a fighter in battle as Maou and Emi, if you ignored the extra boost the Yesod fragments gave Emi and company. If something triggered him into opening hostilities again, Maou had no current way of suppressing him without collateral damage. The presence of Kisaki's feelings was a vital counterweight, and it had to be kept in place to ensure Sariel continued living peacefully in Japan.

This, in other words, was one winning card Maou would never think of actually playing. A card he never really thought of, even, as long as Sariel didn't poke at the hornet's nest too much. In fact, frankly, Sariel's existence or cover story meant very little to Maou compared to the other problems on his mind.

First off, even after that gluttonous trip to MgRonald, Acieth still hadn't really gotten better. This made sense, of course. What was a devastating development in Maou's mind was, to Acieth, just letting herself go a little at dinner. They still didn't know the cause, and they still didn't have a remedy.

Despite that, however, Acieth—perhaps a bit relieved that she had someplace else to be herself—was (apparently) down to about half her appetite at its peak. It was only "apparently" to Maou because he hadn't actually seen her since that day.

Now, more than ever, he was feeling tremendously blocked and boxed up in his life. He had no idea what was motivating Chiho and Suzuno, and now his landlord Shiba and her family were lurking around him, acting undercover in ways he couldn't fathom. He only got updated about Acieth because he happened to catch Nord in front of the apartment building. Being fused with her and all, Maou could forcibly call her over if he wanted to, but he knew she wouldn't really tell him anything, and it's not like he alone could ever provide food on the level to satisfy her appetite.

So Maou had spent the past few days bobbing along, helpless against other people's machinations and left quite in the dark by them all. It put him in a hazy state of depression, one that Emi shared in—her especially, because she had caught wind in Ente Isla of Ashiya, Urushihara, and Gabriel discussing some sort of scheme between them. One week on, and neither of them had heard a single word from Acieth, Suzuno, or Chiho.

Instead, they had other people prowling around:

"Um, good morning."

"Marko!"

Takefumi Kawata was the first to come up to Maou, who was looking glum, as he walked through the automatic doors.

"Wh-what's up, Kawa—"

"There's more weirdoes in here! They gotta be for you, Marko!"

"...Where?"

"Table ten."

"Ohh...ohhh...oh."

Table ten, which Kawata pointed out without turning around, was a stool at the countertop that lined one wall. Three men, backs pointed straight up, were seated at this counter now, their clothing making them look very out of place in Hatagaya.

"S-sorry they keep on doing this. I keep *telling* them to dress right, but..."

"They got in an argument with Libby just now," the almost tearful Kawata said as Maou's shoulders drooped. "He said something about that being formal dress where they come from."

"They don't need to *be* formal, though..."

Maou eyed them. All three men were wearing blue strips of cloth on their left arms.

"What did Ms. Iwaki do?"

"They handed her, like, this solid gold ingot. She's pretty much lost."

"All right. I'll give them a talking-to."

"Please, if you could..."

Leaving Kawata behind, Maou walked up to the three men.

<"Listen, you fools. How many times do I have to tell you before you realize this isn't Ente Isla?">

The tallest of the three men, sitting in the center, turned his eyes to Maou, unperturbed.

<"Satan, the Devil King?">

<"Yes.">

<"Do you know who we are?">

<"Hmm. I don't know anyone who dresses weird and goes around all high-handed like 'Do you know who we are?' So, no.">

<"...!">

One of the other men betrayed his anger for a moment. The tallest one stopped him.

<"...My pardons. We received a report on this land's customs from an advance agent, but as members of the Azure Scarves, we are forbidden from shedding any more equipment than this while on a mission. Understand that coming here unarmed is, in itself, a major concession.">

<"I can't say I really care about your country's rules. You're in Japan right now. The Azure Scarves, the Azure Emperor, the Devil King, the Hero—they're all equally unknown around here. All

you guys are at the moment are strangers, and very weird-looking ones at that. Next time you show up, you better make your country change their rules.">

<"...We'll do our best.">

<"So, if I could ask, what brings you here today...?">

Kawata watched with bated breath, eyeing Maou. "Hopefully this is going well..." Another involved party walked through the automatic door. "Hmm?"

"Good morning! ...Oh."

"Oh! Morning, Yusa."

Emi spotted Maou and the trio immediately. "Good morning, Kawata," she softly said. "Um, those people over there..."

"I don't speak their language so I only have the general gist, but first Libby yelled at them, then Marko lectured them, and I think they're explaining what they're here for now."

"...I'm really sorry about this. Are we still letting customers in?"

"Well, there's not many of them yet, but Ms. Iwaki's freaking out, so maybe you could tend to her for me? Because they gave her this gold bar or something and she doesn't know what to do with it."

"O-okay. Again, sorry!"

"No, um, it's fine by me, but..."

The news that her boss was "freaking out" filled Emi's face with terrified grief. She quickly jogged over to the staff room.

"If it wasn't for all the stuff I'd seen, I would've just assumed they were three weird dudes, but...oh well. Back to work."

With those words to himself, Kawata mentally switched gears and returned to his regular duties.

"Oh, Kawacchi? I just saw Saemi running into the staff room like she saw a ghost, but did something else weird happen?"

Akiko Ohki had just exited the walk-in freezer with a couple bags of food ingredients.

"Marko's handling some out-of-towners right now. Ms. Yusa's helping the boss calm down."

"Why's Ms. Iwaki all worked up? If it's a gold bar, can't she just sell it somewhere?"

"Aki," laughed Kawata, "think a little harder than that, won't you?"

"Well, that's what *I'd* do. Nobody would ever know! It's not like someone from Ente Isla is gonna complain to corporate about it. We could all party it up with the proceeds."

"Talk about dreaming small. That's pretty ethically questionable, Aki—and besides, considering the Devil King of their land took the managerial exam here, you can't totally discount the idea that they'd complain to HQ. No matter how nonsensical it is, embezzling payments is a really bad idea."

"Aww. But Saemi had a job at Dokodemo, didn't she? Maybe Ente Islans have access to phones, too. Like… It's funny how despite all this, life hasn't *really* changed, has it?"

Akiko couldn't sound more indifferent as he loaded the ingredient bags into the kitchen's freezer, the same as she always did.

"*Ahh…* What a pain. Sorry to make you deal with these freaks all the time, Kawacchi."

Maou was back among them now, exhaustion on his face. Before he responded, Kawata looked toward the dining room. The trio were now gone, and the rest of their customers seemed normal enough.

"…Just to be sure, you didn't zap them away with a magic wand or something, right?"

"I don't have one. But if I did and used it that way, Emi would kill me."

"Okay. You know, just in case…"

"Just in case what?"

"Well, as long as they left peaceably, it's all good."

"…Ahh, I haven't even changed yet. Sorry again."

Kawata glanced back at Maou as he hurried into the staff room. He didn't look particularly concerned about anything. By the time Maou clocked in and returned to the floor, a new customer was picking a tray up from Kawata and heading toward the dining hall.

"Kawacchi, where's Libicocco?"

"I got him running the upstairs by himself. Wanna switch out?"

Maou nodded as headed up to the café space. "Sure."

Ever since Chiho had gone off the rails and decided to take Acieth to the MgRonald, the relationship between Maou and his coworker trio of Iwaki, Kawata, and Akiko had changed so little that it actually disappointed him and Emi. Iwaki joking about whether she could start calling him "Your Majesty" or "O Exalted Satan" was the main highlight, but nothing substantial had changed at all. Neither side mentioned the other's origins in conversation or anything—and, as a practical issue, it'd be trouble for all of them if anything *did* change.

This was thanks to Maou's unflagging efforts to build trust in his staff. Once, as they chatted, Kawata mentioned, "You know, I'll just say—it's not like I'm not scared at all." *I'm sure*, Maou thought to that, but then Kawata continued: "But if something was gonna happen because of it, it would've happened a long time ago. So if you guys don't do anything, Marko, it's not like us acting all tense is gonna help."

Maou appreciated Kawata's friendship and analytical skills…but the guilt over having to keep mum about how dangerous it was for everyone when Sariel first came along pained him enough that he bowed his head deeply to him anyway.

The reactions from Akiko, Iwaki, and of course Kisaki were largely the same. Emi and Libicocco had no doubt figured things out with the staff in their own way, too—they hadn't sat down to talk about it or anything, but the two of them didn't seem to act any differently around Iwaki and the rest. Maou had to hand it to them—he had been blessed with a really great workplace.

"…My liege, about Mr. Kawata…"

"Yes?"

Maou looked at Libicocco, who was about to head back downstairs. Then Kawata quietly stuck his head in the stairwell.

"Marko, you got a customer."

"Oh…"

"This one speaks Japanese. He says she's from some church on the 'Western Island'?"

"…Ah…sorry about that."

Behind Kawata was a man wearing flashy robes similar to Suzuno's, someone who clearly wasn't there to nosh on junk food. Maou didn't recognize him, so he probably wasn't involved with their upcoming battle against heaven.

"Again, *why* do you people keep showing up looking like that…?"

"I am under strict orders not to cause offense. These robes are to be worn when only the greatest of respect is to be paid—"

"When you get back," Maou told the robed man, cutting him off, "tell 'em that coming dressed like that is about as *dis*-respectful to me and my coworkers as you can get."

"…I will," the cleric said, not looking very convinced as Maou pointed out the bar seating to him.

"So you're fine for today, but before you leave, do a little street research on how people dress in Japan for me, please? 'Cause if you don't, I'm not going to talk to you again."

"I—I'm afraid I can't have that…"

"Well, tough. I can't have *this*, either, y'know? So which is it?"

"Pardon?"

Maou stared the man down. "Which side are you on? Crestia Bell's, or Cervantes Reberiz's?"

"…I work under the authority of Archbishop Cervantes."

Three members of the Azure Scarves, the most prestigious knighthood of the empire on the Eastern Island, had now been followed by a high-ranking cleric serving one of the Church's six Archbishops. They weren't alone, either. Ever since Maou's and Emi's identities were revealed to the MgRonald staff, the Hatagaya location had seen a pretty constant stream of Ente Isla visitors in unfamiliar dress.

"I'm glad you're being honest. Wait over there for me, okay? I'll talk to you when I get some time… Ah!"

Maou sternly addressed the cleric, pointing out the seat farthest away from the upstairs entrance for him to sit on. He then ran over to Kawata, hands clasped together and head down.

"I'm really sorry! I know this is asking a lot, but the next time someone like this shows up, can you point them in Emi's direction?"

"...Yeah, that's fine, but...Marko?"

"Huh?"

"I think that before their clothing, you need to teach them about our currency system. With the clothes, you know, no matter how weird they are, if they sit down and keep quiet, it's no biggie, right? But if they keep paying us with gold bars and jewels and stuff, it'll just make Ms. Iwaki more flustered, and I'm not sure Aki's just joking about taking it all to the pawn shop anymore. It's really got us all on edge."

"I'm *really* sorry about this!"

Maou was in full apology mode now, the cleric looking on wide-eyed like he was viewing cataclysmic events. "Everyone who comes here gets a surprise like that," Libicocco observed with a smirk.

"Wh-what?"

"You had best be careful, human," he continued, addressing the Church cleric. "If you anger the staff here, neither His Demonic Highness nor the Hero Emilia will lend their ears to you again."

"I—I will be sure not to...um, but may I ask who you are...?"

"Me? I am Libicocco, Malebranche chieftain in the Devil King's Army. Let me inform you that all the humans in this restaurant are aware of that, and I am *still* serving at the lowest rung on the ladder here. I'd thus advise you to watch your behavior and your mouth."

The cleric gulped nervously, then quickly made his way to the seat Maou pointed out for him. If a place like this treated a Malebranche chief who once laid waste to vast swaths of Ente Isla's Southern Island as a proverbial cabin boy, there was no telling how powerful everyone *else* must be. It must have scared the pants off of him.

"But everyone here seems very obedient, I must say," Libicocco noted to Maou. "Should I take it to mean that things are going well with Chiho Sasaki?"

"No comment."

Libicocco chuckled a bit while Maou scowled, before nodding his good-byes and heading downstairs.

"Things are going well...?"

Really, what was going well and what wasn't? Maou wasn't sure any longer. After all, a constant stream of powerful Ente Islan figures were rushing into the MgRonald by Hatagaya Station, asking essentially the same question.

But why were they here?

It was all Chiho and Suzuno planning out this so-called "Second Invasion" of Devil's Castle. The humans, who would only be aware of this plan on the surface at best, probably couldn't even imagine what was going on…and truth be told, Maou and Emi, too, were having trouble keeping up with it.

✱

The first one to come knocking was no shock to Maou, Emi, or even Libicocco.

This was someone whose presence bumbling around Japan was no great surprise. But this person still startled Emi, because she picked up on something unusual very quickly. After all, this person should've been well-versed in modern Japanese culture by now… and yet, she still chose to dress like *that* at MgRonald.

"Hellooo, good afternooooon!"

"E-Eme?! What the heck are you wearing?!"

It was Emeralda Etuva: companion to the Hero in her Devil King–slaying quest, chief figure in the upcoming battle against heaven, and Emi's closest friend. She had enjoyed an extended stay at Emi's apartment in Eifukucho and understood the norms of Japanese society by now—so why was she wearing the ceremonial robes of a palace conjurer from the Holy Empire of Saint Aile?

"Oh, don't be meeean…"

"…Eme?"

Emi noticed something odd with Emeralda's face. It seemed calm and composed on the surface, but her eyes, her mouth—the full range of her expression—was only about half the amplitude it usually was. And based on her experience, Emi was reasonably sure what this meant: Emeralda was angry about something.

The surprised exclamation from Emi must've made it up the stairs, because when Maou came down from the café space to answer it, he was greeted by the sorcerer's guileful eyes looking straight up at him.

"Hello there, Devil King Satan."

The voice sharpened itself toward the end. Emi nervously gulped. There was something on Emeralda's mind that made her seethe.

"E-Emeralda?! What're you doing dressed like that…?" he asked.

"You and Emilia seem rather preoccupied with my wardrobe, don't you? Is it that strange?"

"Well, I mean…"

"I am here to offer my greetings to the manager of this restaurant, on behalf of the Holy Empire of Saint Aile and, by extension, all the peoples of Ente Isla. If I were to visit here dressed in a manner that hid myself amid your own culture, wouldn't that itself be rude?"

"Wh-what are you…?"

"Ahh, I have no time to spend being bothered by these charlatans. Emilia—where may I find Ms. Iwaki?"

"Hey!" Maou yelled.

"Huh? Um…huh? Eme?" Emi stammered. "I'm sorry, I'm not sure I'm really following, myself…"

"…Um, something up?"

Iwaki, picking up on the strife in the dining space, appeared from the kitchen. Emeralda, quickly spotting her, walked up, took a knee, and lowered her head.

"U-Um, madam? Y-you *are* a guest, right? In more ways than one?!"

"Eme! Hey! There's other people here!"

Iwaki, being a grown woman and having experienced Chiho's huge revelation, must have known something was unusual about all this.

"You are Ms. Kotomi Iwaki? I have come from Ente Isla, the Land of the Holy Cross, as a palace representative from the Holy Empire of—"

"Ex…Ex-*cuse* me, madam, but if we could perhaps continue this conversation in my office?!"

Iwaki moved quickly. She grabbed the arm of Emeralda, a woman about the same size as she.

"Libby! Meet me in the back!"

"Right!"

"...of Saint Aiiiile..."

Nimbly giving the signal to Libicocco, who was watching from behind the counter, Iwaki pulled Emeralda out of public sight, evacuating them both into the staff room. Left behind in all this was Emi, Maou, Akiko (who had a vague idea what was going on), and the rest of the crew handling the shift (who didn't).

"Um, let's, let's just get back to work, people..."

Maou used his authority as the substitute floor manager on duty to get everyone's heads out of the clouds. But Akiko wasn't ready to fold.

"Was she...one of *those* people?" she whispered.

Emi nodded. "Yes, but...but she's never done anything like *this* before... Ah."

Then she heard the front doors whirring open, forcing her mind back into MgRonald employee mode.

"Good afternoo—*npph?!*"

She wound up biting her tongue.

This time, a man came through the door, a tall figure in a long, overelaborate robe with sharp, ambitious eyes. Why would he appear in a place like this? Even Maou tensed up at the sight.

"How nice to see you again, Emilia the Hero. I am sure even God above couldn't have imagined us encountering each other in such a manner. I am glad you seem to remain well."

"Ar...Archbishop Cervantes... Wh-why...?"

This man, one of the six Archbishops, stood at the peak of power and faith in the Church bureaucracy. He was someone who, no matter how chaotic this timeline had become, would never walk through the doors of a western Tokyo MgRonald in broad daylight.

Cervantes, firmly in control of the situation, gave the dining space a good look. Then his eyes settled upon Maou, currently frozen in the middle of the staircase.

"And…yes. I can hardly believe my eyes."

"I'm having trouble believing mine, too…"

The Archbishop probably had trouble accepting that Satan, the Devil King, was now a young Japanese man. Emi, meanwhile, couldn't believe Cervantes was right here, in front of her, and completely unaccompanied.

As the de facto leader of the six Archbishops, Cervantes Reberiz was (in Maou's and Emi's minds) a puppet of the heavenly realm and the greatest enemy of humankind on Ente Isla. If the head Archbishop came to learn about Japan, not to mention the truth behind the Devil King's Army, then one nod of his head could very feasibly trigger a world war pitting every force in Ente Isla against the Devil King's Army within the space of an hour. He was the last person they wanted to know about their assault on heaven, or even that Emi was alive at all. So why was he planet-hopping to MgRonald without a single Church knight to guard him?

"…I do not have much time. I have been warned not to cause too much commotion in this world. For today, I have come to size up the leader of this…*establishment*, where the Hero and Devil King work."

"Huh?!"

"Is Ms. Kotomi Iwaki or Ms. Mayumi Kisaki present?"

What informant even gave him those names, the names of those MgRonald managers Archbishop Cervantes was now gravely intoning? It gave Emi a dizzy spell.

"Ah, um, Iwaki is currently attending to another guest…"

"Another guest? Then my apologies, but I will wait."

Without awaiting a reply, Cervantes sat himself down at a nearby empty seat. Then he closed his eyes, as if meditating, not moving an inch as Maou, Emi, and Akiko stood there at a loss.

"Wh-what's with *that*, Emi?! What's going on?!"

"I don't know! I didn't think Lord Cervantes would come here… W-wait a minute!"

She had heard the name Cervantes somewhere recently. Right. It was…

"Oh, wow, Chiho…"

"Huh?" Maou blinked in confusion.

Akiko faced the confused pair, looking even more confused herself. "Um, Saemi, Maou, it's looking kind of like…"

Then Emeralda appeared from the staff room. Cervantes's eyes immediately opened, staring intently at Emeralda's back as she bowed back at the doorway to the manager's office. Then, chin up, back straight, she walked right over to Cervantes's seat, like she'd always known he was there.

"How nice to see you."

"Yes. Sorry about the other day."

It was a short greeting, but one as willful and tactical as a physical swordfight.

"Do not worry. I am simply here as her friend."

"What a coincidence. I am an old acquaintance of hers as well, and that's what brings me here."

"Is it, now?"

"Yes."

"…Then thank you for taking time out of your busy schedule to come, Father Reberiz."

"Ah, yes. Miss Etuva, I know how occupied we both are, but we in the Church have yet to make up for our affront upon you and your nation. Would you like to perhaps share a meal together?"

"My, what a kind invitation. It would be an honor, Father Reberiz. In fact, why don't we do just that right now?"

"Now? Here?"

Even Cervantes looked visibly astonished. Emeralda just sweetly smiled back.

"Were you not aware? Occupying a seat without ordering anything is considered poor table manners in this nation."

"I see. In that case…"

After looking around himself once more, Cervantes wearily stood up, turning first to Emi, then to Maou.

"In that case, should I provide an order to them in their servant capacities? I still lack knowledge in the ways of other worlds, Miss Etuva. Would you be able to teach me a little about the culture here?"

"I am glad to be of service. Being able to dine with one of the six Archbishops is almost too great an honor for any adherent to the faith."

So the two state figures walked up to the order counter. Emi and Maou stood frozen in the dining space, unsure what to do, while Iwaki and Libicocco were still in the staff room. This left only Akiko manning the registers.

"M-may—may—may I help you?"

Maou and Emi had nothing but praise for the way Akiko managed to handle these two extremely atypical customers. In another few moments, the Archbishop and the palace enchanter were facing each other over a small table, working on their respective regular burgers, small fries, and small iced coffees—at 350 yen, one of the simplest combos.

It was a surreal sight, but impressively enough, everyone in the restaurant except for Maou, Emi, and Akiko quickly turned their attention elsewhere. The aura this pair emitted was like nothing any sane, decent couple would show, after all, and their clothing was beyond strange. But Mayumi Kisaki had drilled into everyone on staff that anyone who paid money to eat here was a customer, and Kotomi Iwaki's crew had taken on that mandate.

Most of the employees no longer focused on the pair, seeing them as a bit uncommon but nothing more. The same was true of the other customers. Live long enough in Tokyo, and it wasn't rare to see people with pretty eccentric tastes in their clothing. As long as they weren't acting too far outside the norms of society, they were accepted as part of the diversity the world offered—one advantage of being in such an international city. Along those lines, it was Maou and Emi who were acting weird here, fully aware of what was going on.

Once they wrapped up their meal, Cervantes looked at the paper wrappers left on his tray and smiled a bit.

"You never know what you'll experience in life, do you? That was quite an attractive meal, Miss Etuva."

"I agree. This 'MgRonald' is one of the most renowned restaurants in this world. I am sure everyone at your headquarters would be equally appreciative."

"I should hope so, yes. By the way, the currency from this nation I saw earlier…"

Emeralda stopped cold at the observation. The Japanese yen she had on her was borrowed from Emi, back during her stay on Earth before the whole heaven-invasion plan kicked off. With their meal costing seven hundred yen total, she had just three hundred of it left—a fact she kept a secret for now.

"Please, Father Reberiz, allow me the honor of providing an Archbishop with a free meal today."

In other words, Emeralda was treating him, so stop bothering her about it.

"…I will gladly accept that, then." Cervantes nodded, understanding what she meant and dropping the subject. "Indeed, I have my own business to settle presently, so please forgive me for taking my leave at this time. I shall repay the favor sometime."

"Yes, of course."

With that, Cervantes stood and walked straight for a very disheartened-looking Iwaki, now back on the floor and on duty. When she noticed all the majesty of his approaching figure, a look of desperation came to her face as she realized the fate awaiting her a minute or so from now.

"E-Eme…"

"It's not going to end like thiiis, you know," Emeralda told Emi as she watched the Archbishop go.

"…Huh?"

"She certainly has some pretty crazy ideas running through her head, doesn't sheee? Honestly, I'm not much of a faaan. It's straying rather farrr from our initial plans."

"Y-you mean…?"

Emi recalled the other day, when Chiho had brought her MgRonald friends to the Northern Island for a quick trip.

"Does this have to do with the conference Chiho is chairing?"

"Do you think it doooesn't?" came the slightly disgusted reply.

"Well, you say that," Maou added, "but remember, *we're* completely out of the loop, too! Neither Chi, nor Ashiya, nor Suzuno has told us anything. What the hell is going on?"

"Don't give me that craaap," Emeralda said, blowing off Maou's complaints. "Yes, it was the plan all along to leave you two in Japaaan, but not informing you about something as important as thiiis makes no sense to me. All riiight? So listen."

The truth, as Emeralda laid it out, was far more serious than either of them anticipated.

"The other day, Chief Dhin Dhem Wurs and Archbishop Crestia Bell released a secret communiqué signed by the both of them. It described their desire to hold a summit to address the rancor in the Central Continent and debate over the general future of the world. The missive included a full list of invitees. They included me, Rumack, Lord Cervantes, the Azure Emperor, and Chief Rajid Rahs Rian. And…"

The next moment, Maou and Emi almost fainted on the MgRonald floor.

"…the summit will be chaired by Great Demon General Chiho Sasaki of the Devil King's Army. She signed the missive herself, in Japanese and everything. Am I making this clear to you? The fact that you can't be left in the dark any longer?"

Emeralda's severe eyes all but overwhelmed Maou and Emi.

"Chiho's attempting to have us engineer this farce called the 'Second Invasion' of Devil's Castle. A show the entire world will join in. She's trying to create a stage where the Devil King's Army and Ente Isla's human forces settle matters without shedding a drop of blood. Only she would attempt such an insane, needle-threading endeavor."

✻

After Emeralda and Cervantes's visit, dignitaries from across Ente Isla continued to stop by the Hatagaya Station MgRonald on practically a daily basis. In most cases, first a leader or someone correspondingly powerful would arrive; then a stream of aides would come along—not doing anything per se, but simply visiting the MgRonald, saying hello to Maou, Emi, and Iwaki, then leaving. As Emeralda put it, they wanted to keep watch over Emilia the Hero, making sure she didn't get swayed into one faction or the other.

All this was conducted with perfect politeness. Nobody tried anything untoward, like the Eight Scarves of the past—if they did, they'd be denounced at the summit, and the names of the Azure Emperor, Rajid, and Cervantes apparently had enough force to keep them all in check.

With the Church calling for a Crusade, all sides could see the chaos threatening to unfold on the Central Continent. Everyone also knew that, should the Church use this "Crusade" to deploy knights across the continent, the Azure Emperor of Efzahan wouldn't take that quietly. Both sides, of course, hoped to avoid the futility of an across-the-board clash; they just wanted to occupy the continent and reap the benefits. And now this summit was dropping into the middle of it all.

Dhin Dhem Wurs, heralded as the greatest chief herder to ever lead the Northern Island, oversaw a government whose power was acknowledged on the world stage. Neither East nor West wanted to make an enemy out of such an influential Northern figure. To the Church knight corps, the "Crusade" pretext meant they preferred keeping any casualties to an absolute minimum, and to the Eight Scarves, although they wanted to rule over the Central Continent someday, diving into a hasty invasion in the face of this Crusade would leave them ill-prepared.

As Emeralda explained, Chiho had declared this summit with the goal of avoiding excess bloodshed around the invasion of heaven—and this was being cased around the pretext of the "Second Invasion" of Devil's Castle. This invasion was what Chiho was sharing with all the related parties; it let her create an environment where all the world's top commanders could calm down and constructively work together—something that should benefit Maou and his cohorts on Earth. Otherwise, the Shiba family wouldn't take this sitting down—they'd take it out on everyone involved, Maou included. To Maou, however, it felt like having to walk a tightrope he didn't want anything to do with, in the middle of a dense fog. It was nothing that'd calm his fears at all.

For today, at least, the line of Ente Islan visitors ended with a bishop apparently under Cervantes's command. By the time the shift wrapped up, both Maou and Emi were at the end of their mental ropes. They had, after all, put Iwaki, Kawata, and Akiko through the wringer all day. Iwaki brushed it off, saying, "It's fine, I'm used to this," but Maou and Emi both swore to themselves not to rely on her good graces. If someone involved with this summit decided to cause harm to MgRonald or anything around it, there'd be no way they could ever make up for that.

"…It hasn't felt this way in a while, huh?" Emi said as they walked home after closing.

"What do you mean?"

"This…pins-and-needles feeling. Like you don't even know what's gonna happen an hour from now."

"What, has anything that tense happened recently?"

She glared at Maou, who was walking his bicycle next to her. "I'm talking about right after we first met each other. In Sasazuka."

Of course, ever since he started calling himself Sadao Maou, he hadn't demonstrated any of the evil tyranny Emi had initially imagined. But—picturing how she must've felt at the time—there was no telling what the Devil King Satan might attempt. It must've cost her a lot of sleep in the beginning.

"…Well, thanks. Man, I'm hungry. Wonder what's for dinner. Maybe it's *yakisoba* again…"

And if *that's* where she wanted to take the subject, Maou had to go hands-off with it fast. So he decided to imagine what Libicocco, who left work at ten PM earlier, might be cooking for him.

"But compared to then, at least I know I can go to bed in peace. So there's that."

"How do you know that? Think about what the Eight Scarves did to Ashiya and Rika Suzuki. Who knows what kind of crap they could pull right now…"

"I doubt it. I mean, think about it—ever since Eme and Cervantes showed up, we haven't had more than one faction come visit at the same time, right? And nobody's come knocking at *our* doors."

"Yeah, true."

"If I had to guess, someone's probably regulating their coming and going. You said it yourself—Tiferet on Earth *did* something to you. I don't know who's serving as a go-between for everyone in Ente Isla, but I'm sure Ms. Shiba or Amane are helping regulate traffic, so to speak."

"Well, I wish they'd stop pointing them at our workplace."

"…I think this is better, actually. I feel bad for our coworkers, but…"

"What?"

"Like, if they came to your or my place, maybe whatever *they're* worried about might actually happen, you know? One of us getting kidnapped, or something."

"I wouldn't let them."

"That's not the point. I'm not a hundred percent sure of this or anything…but when they get sent to MgRonald, they see us acting subservient to our manager. They see coworkers with the same social status as us."

"…Oh."

Come to think of it, Libicocco used similar wording to threaten that guy from the Church.

"So this arrangement limits their options, you know? If they try anything rash, they risk angering us—and for all they know, maybe there's someone crazy powerful on our side in there. Any bets they make along those lines offer tons of risk and not much return."

"Ah… Of course, I'm sure that makes Cervantes wonder even more what all this summit crap is about. Every other player in this game's colluding with each other in one way or another, so I can see if they're taking it slow."

"But seeing him come along right after Eme… I have to hand it to her. If she let Cesar or Mauro come visit, it wouldn't have turned out like that, I don't think."

"Yeah, well, I don't know what any of them are really thinking apart from Suzuno, so…um, you know, it's all the same to me."

Maou paused for a moment, then sighed. There was no sound for a while, apart from the creaking of Dullahan II's chain as it rotated around.

"Hmm… So did you give Bell an answer?"

"……………………Give me a break."

He hoped Emi would let that pause slide. He was playing with the wrong girl.

"Isn't that something you keep secret until it gets worked out? I mean, what's that idiot even thinking?"

With Chiho, there wasn't much he could do. But if you told someone you loved him and the guy immediately ran away without replying, that wasn't the sort of thing he wanted to discuss on end afterward.

Emi, picking up on this, scowled. "Well, *that's* a mean way to put it."

"For a cleric, she sure ain't shy about blabbing about it to everyone, apparently."

"If something's bothering a cleric, she's obligated to confess it to someone."

"Oh, yeah, go ahead, bring religion into it! Don't make her the hero of this. What kind of life have you led if you think it's okay for a cleric to react like *that*?"

The slightly incoherent ranting was followed by a sharp gaze thrown in Emi's direction.

"When did she tell you? On the way back from Ente Isla with Ms. Kisaki and everyone?"

"Pretty much."

"You sure sat on it for a while."

"Well, I've had my hands full. Plus, this is totally different from you and Chiho."

The pair began walking again as the light in front of them turned green.

"If you don't mind me saying," he continued, "that whole thing was an accident anyway. I dunno how much you heard, but I've got no interest in hearing you people whine at me about it."

"Why are you acting so defensive? I'm not whining at you."

Even so, Emi couldn't help but smile a bit at Maou as he continued rattling off his grievances.

"But, you know," she continued, "my first impression when I heard…"

"Quit it."

"…was, you know, you're *really* weak at the pivotal moment, aren't you?"

"…Jerk."

Emi couldn't help but smile from ear to ear at Maou as he gritted his teeth.

"Devil King?"

"Shut up."

"Someone's there."

"I know."

It was on the other end of the Hatagaya darkness—on the Koshu-Kaido road, a well-trafficked street with ample illumination. Both of them could feel something out there, remorselessly watching them.

"They sure make a show out of taking action, huh? Did someone unrelated smell them out?"

"If so, they sure don't seem too careful. Because I spotted them right out… Hmm? Huh? Whoa, wait…"

Suddenly, Emi stopped, frantically looking around. Then:

"N-no!"

A small, glowing light appeared in her chest, followed by a small, light *pop*, like a tiny balloon.

"E-Emi?! Was that Alas Ramus…?"

It was the sound Alas Ramus made whenever she manifested herself. It was getting close to midnight.

"Maybe her stomach hurts or something?"

"She... She sometimes cries a little at night, but hardly at all lately... Huh? Alas Ramus?" Emi's voice shook in her confusion. "...Where are you?"

"What?"

The arms she usually held out to catch her manifested "daughter" seemed unusually light. It scared her. But it wasn't until Maou noticed something solid clanking to her feet that he realized what was the matter.

"It... It's just her clothing?"

All that was in Emi's hands was the dress she'd put on the girl this morning.

At her feet were Alas Ramus's favorite Relax-a-Bear water bottle, a bag of cookies, and another bag with a change of clothes for the child.

"H-how did you take her clothes off her? ...Also, you can store *stuff* inside you, too?"

Maou was impressed, although now wasn't the time for it. Emi, meanwhile, quickly turned pale.

"She's gone... She's not here!"

"Huh?"

"Alas Ramus is the only thing not here! She had her clothes and that bottle on her!"

"...What? You sure she didn't tear her clothes off while she was sleeping or something?"

Emi couldn't say if that was possible in her fused state, but she shook her head at Maou, who was still concerning himself with irrelevant matters.

"I'd know if she was fused with me! You can, too, right?! Alas Ramus?! Alas Ramus, where are you?!"

Emi searched for the little girl, who was nowhere in sight. Whoever was watching her a moment ago was no longer on her mind.

"Ch-chill a second. Just fuse back with her..."

"I'm trying to! I can't!"

"Shit, really?"

Now Maou was finally understanding the weight of the situation.

He picked up the bottle and clothing bag as he looked around. There was no way Alas Ramus could ever be lost. But Emi wasn't agitated simply because something unexpected had happened.

"Oh, no... Did she do something...?!"

She recalled how it felt when Alas Ramus was taken from her arms. It happened deep beneath the demon realms, where she attempted to fend off a strange foe in a space suit and failed. Sephirah were capable of undoing fused states if they were touching each other. Emi felt connected to her at the core, something that brought an absolute sort of comfort to her—and now that, along with Emi's heart, was brutally shaken.

"...Mm?"

Then Maou noticed something.

"Emi! Calm down! It's still all right!"

"What's all right?! Devil King! Let's split up and—"

"You can still *try* to merge with her, right? That means you're still connected!"

"...!"

That calmed her, if only a little bit.

"She hasn't been taken or anything. Alas Ramus's consciousness is still connected to yours. I know we never imagined this...but she really *is* just lost, out there somewhere!"

"You...you think so?"

"That's the only explanation! Just use an Idea Link or whatever else you can think of to grab her attention! I'll wake up Nord and Amane and have them help look for her! ...Damn, if only Ashiya or Suzuno were around!"

Maou whipped out his phone as he griped to himself. Emi, watching him, wiped her teary eyes, took a deep breath, and mentally reset her mind.

"...Alas Ramus, where did you go?!"

No answer. She was nowhere to be seen. But they were still connected.

"Devil King! I'm gonna go scope out the vicinity!"

"Okay! I'll..." Maou looked around, confirming that Alas Ramus was nowhere within sight. Then he turned toward the presence they felt before. "I'll go chase after that Peeping Tom!"

"All right."

Someone was still watching them—a figure that may just be involved in this.

He focused on that presence as he called Nord and gave him the rundown. "Hello? Sorry I'm calling so late! We got an emergency! I can't say for sure, but she may be trying to walk to the apartment building, so keep an eye out! …Okay. Now for Amane…"

Fresh off the phone with Nord, he brought up his directory again to call up Amane—

"Whoa!"

But then Amane called him instead, making his eyes go wide.

"Hello, Amane? We actually got some trouble right now… Huh?"

Maou couldn't understand what he was being told at first. But if she called him to say it, it couldn't have been meaningless.

"Hey, Emi!" he shouted, as she ran off in the opposite direction.

"What?"

"Hang on! She's over there!"

"…Huh?!"

"Alas Ramus is there!"

"Wh-where?!"

She came thundering back to Maou, who looked incredulous himself as he pointed at the phone glued to his ear.

"…She's sleeping with Acieth at my landlord's place."

And not even Emi had anything to counter that with.

※

It was one in the morning as a haggard-looking Maou and Emi watched Alas Ramus sleep in Acieth's bed, the sound of Acieth enjoying a midnight snack in the background. Having her show up without any clothing worried them, but for some reason, she had a yellow dress on now—one Emi thought she had stored in a clothes drawer in her apartment.

None of this made sense, but regardless, Emi sat on the floor, filled with relief that the little girl was safe. Maou, for his part, felt tormented. He hated going to Shiba's house in the first place, but the idea that unknown Earth Sephirah might be lying in wait for him inside worried him. They never did chase down that weird presence; it had been gone by the time they'd reached the Shiba residence.

"Wow, Maou, you look the very sick!"

"I feel very sick. In more ways than one."

"Oh yeah?"

"How are you not getting an upset stomach?"

"I dunno."

Leaving the nonchalant Acieth behind, Maou and Emi turned to Amane, herself looking troubled.

"Well, it sounds like you've had a busy night, but we were all scared outta our wits here, lemme tell ya," Amane said. "This super-bright light poured out of the room, and I thought, y'know, maybe this was it—maybe Acieth was finally gonna explode."

"That is the very rude, Amane!"

No one could blame Amane. Acieth was away from her peak, but even now, she was still working her way through thirty rice balls overnight, and any hunger pangs immediately brought out death rays from her face. She was able to sleep at night, apparently, because they let her use the room she usually crashed in whenever she stayed at Shiba's house, but the damage on the walls was in plain sight for all to see.

"So, Amane…," Maou began.

"Hmm?"

"What's going on?"

"Well, that's not really the right question. Shouldn't it be more like 'What do *you* think's going on?'"

"I have a lot of other things I want to ask about, so…"

Maou's firmness made Amane size up everyone in the room.

"Well, I *am* sorry we haven't been in contact much lately," she said.

"That's not what I'm talking about."

"Now hear me out. The whole thing with Chiho earlier might have something to do with Acieth right now. That, and why Alas Ramus is doing something she's never done before."

"Amane, what do you know?" Emi asked, voice stricken with grief.

Amane frowned deeply. "Let me just say, it's not like we know anything, either. We're making suppositions based on past experience, but there's no guarantee we're right. That's why we had Uncle George come over, since he happened to be available."

"Uncle George?"

"You met him, didn't you, Maou? He's my uncle. Or maybe you'd know him better as the Tiferet of Earth?"

"Ah!"

Maou recalled the blond-haired man who had used some... *method* to stop him from storming into Shiba's house the day before Chiho and Suzuno went all haywire.

"That bastard... Was that him just now, too...?"

He found it all quite distasteful, but was that the presence he'd felt? Not murderous or hostile—just kind of there, dogging Maou around his neighborhood but never trying to make contact? Was that fishy-looking guy behind it?

"I'll leave that to your imagination," Amane said, seeming to read Maou's mind. "But as for this, I don't know if it's a good change or a bad one. Aunt Mikitty thinks it's a good one, but now Chiho's involved with this, and she's a human from our world. We can't say anything careless to her, and to be honest, there's a lot I just don't know. Binah's my dad, after all, not me."

"Listen," Emi said, "I'm not asking you about all the great mysteries of the world or anything. I'm just worried about Alas Ramus."

"I hear you." Amane nodded. "So just listen to me. What did Chiho try to do? What happened as a result, and what *will* happen? What's the deal with Acieth, and with Alas Ramus just now? ...Well, at this point, I doubt Alas Ramus will wake up at all tonight, so..."

She beckoned Maou and Emi to follow her out of the room.

"Let's talk over some tea in the living room, huh? And I think you'll want to be sitting down for it, so... Acieth, can you take care of your big sister for me?"

"You got it! On job now!"

Proceeding down a dim hallway, the two of them sat down on a sofa in a living room decked out in thick, clashing colors and patterns. Amane broke out some teacups, a thermos full of hot water, and a set of store-brand teabags. "It's late and all," she apologized, as she prepared two cups of tea for them both.

"So as for why Chiho tried doing what she did… Well, there a lot of factors, but first, I want to ask you two something."

"Yes?"

"What is it…?"

"Do you remember back when Urushihara unleashed his attack on Sasazuka?"

"Huh?"

"Well, sure…"

It was an incident they'd never forget—Urushihara, instigated by Olba, launching a full-blown terror attack on Japan in order to kill Maou and Emi. They mulled over it a little.

"And…that's when she learned about Ente Isla. That I'm the Hero, and he's the Devil King?"

"Mmm, you're close."

"Yeah, and back then, my default plan was to erase the memories of anyone who found out about us."

"Ah, getting colder now."

"…So what is it?"

Amane nodded to herself, placed her cup down…

"You know, when you join adulthood, it gets really hard to make friends."

…then bounded off into another tangent.

"I mean, you can make acquaintances really easily, right? At work, or in your private life. But once you start making your own money and learn a little more about the world, it gets overwhelmingly harder to make friends than back in childhood."

Was this some kind of metaphor? As they gave her befuddled stares, Amane asked them an even more confusing question.

"For example… Well, how much do you make a year, Maou?"

"Huh?!"

It was an astoundingly sudden thing to ask.

"Wh-where did *that* come from?!"

"Don't want me to ask you? You worked an entire year last year, right?"

"It, it's not that, but... I mean, I can tell you, but..."

"By the way," Amane added, "I made a little less than three million yen last year, I think."

"Oh, please, don't tell me..."

Talking about one's salary was always a delicate subject for grown-ups.

"But...yeah, sounds like you have trouble saying it. So let me ask you instead, Yusa..."

"Y-yes?"

"Have you ever had a boyfriend before?"

"Huhh?!"

"Like, any of the boys back in your village? Did you ever say you loved someone, or vice versa?"

"N-no! Nothing at all like that! Why are you asking *that* out of nowhere?!"

"Mmm, yeah, sounds like you're telling the truth. By the time I was *your* age, Yusa, I probably had three or so boys say that to me, but..."

It was nothing anyone in the room needed to know...and besides, it was just as delicate a topic to explore. The two of them shuddered to think what Amane may ask next...but as they did, she changed the subject again.

"So can you talk to your adult friends about either of those things?"

""I...It's not impossible, but...,"" they both said.

Topics like money and romance are double-edged swords, great ways to chisel cracks in any human relationship. But they still had no idea how that connected to Chiho's behavior.

"But I'm sure Chiho and her friends talk about this stuff, don't they?"

"What do you mean?"

"Like, how much money they got over the holiday season, or how much their allowance is, or what they made off their part-time jobs. They talk about that all the time, even if they're not particularly close friends at all. Girls gossip with each other about who's been seen with which guy—they get all giggly over this stuff grown women would never talk about…although I guess guys do, huh? Even after graduating from college. Like, there's always one guy who brags about how much he won in pachinko or horse racing, or brings up the average salaries of this or that company…"

Amane winced a bit, as if recalling a bad memory. Then she shook it off, looking back at Maou and Emi.

"But, you know, we usually stop talking about that stuff pretty early on in life, and we stop asking about it. That makes it easier to build relationships, and honestly, it's nothing we *need* to know anyway. But that's exactly the kind of stuff you talked about with Chiho. You built this *special* kind of relationship, based on secrets you wouldn't normally tell other people. Turn that around, and you're all friends who can tell each other anything, no matter what. And… you know, maybe you haven't lived in Japan long enough to understand this, but it's kind of miraculous. All the money in the world wouldn't buy that. Sometimes you can live your whole life without running into anyone like that. And Chiho…"

Amane looked at Maou, Emi, and then Villa Rosa Sasazuka, visible through the living-room window.

"…You know, Chiho's been having dinner with people like that all the time."

"…!"

"You guys never erased Chiho's memory. And I've always been thinking about why, and the only reason I can think of is because you wanted Chiho to remember both of you. You saw Chiho as someone special, and you treated her that way. I'm sure she picked up on that, and you *know* how much she has the hots for you, right, Maou? That's bound to make you real happy, isn't it?"

"What exactly do you mean by 'the hots'?"

Maou couldn't help but harp on Amane's choice of words.

"But, again, turn that around, and it also means you've been pushing your own agenda on her. You know what I mean? You put all these deep, heavy secrets on the mind of a child."

"I...I have regretted that, yes," Emi said. "But Chiho accepted that, and now that we've been relying on her for so long... Was that why?"

"Well, sure, I know she's really important to you. You cared for her, in your own kinda way. And Chiho was just trying to do the same to you. The whole thing."

"...What do you mean?"

"Chiho really loves you guys. You're incredibly precious to her. Not just you, Maou, but Yusa and Ashiya and Kamazuki and Urushihara—the idea of never seeing any of you again is something she wants to avoid at all costs. You built this relationship with her where you don't have to hide your true selves, and she built a relationship with *you* where she doesn't have to hide her desire to be around you forever. Although I guess it was Kamazuki who triggered that..."

"Bell?"

"...!"

Emi's eyes opened wide in surprise. Maou's body tensed up, watching Emi with just her eyes. Amane, noticing this, grinned.

"And you *knoooow*, I wondered why someone as impassive as Kamazuki would go so far out of her way to help Chiho again like that. Right? Not that *I'd* ever know..."

Like hell you don't, Maou thought. He was sure of it. And Suzuno's loose lips made him want to scream out loud all over again, no matter who was with him.

"But it sounds like Chiho, you know, thought that you'd all have to leave Japan once you defeat God and help the Sephirah out."

"That..."

That's not true, Emi was about to say, but she quickly fell silent. Things in Ente Isla might be even more unstable right now than back when the Devil King's Army appeared. This was chiefly thanks to the Church's Crusade, but even ignoring that, the invasion of heaven brought along with it the potential powder keg of demons permanently residing on the planet. The Central Continent was already alive with conflict over who was contributing the most to its rebuilding, and Efzahan was far from the only nation with designs upon expanding their territory.

Would Maou and everyone be able to live in Japan like before once their invasion was over? No. That could never happen. Maou and Ashiya would have to run around handling the demons settling worldwide—and since Urushihara was physically incapable of caring for himself, he couldn't stay in Japan, either. Suzuno and Emeralda, as some of the precious few arbitrators who could work between humans and demons, would have to go fulfill that role as well. And as for Emi and Alas Ramus…

"Yusa, if someone told you to choose between Chiho or Alas Ramus, which one would you pick?"

The question was beyond malicious. Alas Ramus wasn't connected to Emi by blood. But still…

"Chiho, you know, is aware of everything you're dealing with. *All* of it. And she's trying so hard to match up your hopes, and your roles, with her own hopes. She's trying to pull you all into this world where you solve all of Ente Isla's problems peacefully and she can have dinner with you guys anytime she wants. I get reports in from Ashiya and Kamazuki and Emeralda regularly, but she's working crazy hard with all these dignitaries over there."

Amane turned to Maou, looking deadly serious.

"Maou, I'm sorry if I'm being too pushy, but you're never gonna find another kid as well-put-together as her—no matter how hard you look. So if you just keep bumping along like you are now, she's gonna see how shallow you are, and she's gonna dump you like yesterday's news, okay?"

"Dump me? I…"

"And this is exactly why you can't even deal with Kamazuki, either!"

Maou winced, despite claiming to know nothing about her three minutes earlier.

Even Emi didn't seem to see it coming. "You didn't do something to Bell, did you?" she asked, side-eyeing him.

"I—I didn't do anything," Maou replied weakly.

"Oh, right, yeah," Amane said, tone thick with judgment. "It's more what was done *to* him, right? Not that Maou himself can do anything…"

"Amane, you're pushing my buttons here!"

He had to raise his voice, not wanting Emi to know about any more of this. But it just mired him deeper in the swamp. Emi was still giving him looks; it was easy to imagine that she still doubted him.

"Well…I mean, I know why Chi did what she did. I really do. And I can appreciate how we're partly to blame for that. It's not like we told her to never tell anyone, either."

"Right, yeah. And I don't think I said that to Rika, either."

Nobody would believe their stories anyway—if all they did was tell them about it. That piece of insurance was what got them this far…and that made Maou think of something.

"Ah…"

"Huh?"

"…Oh, right… I never apologized to Chi's mom."

"…Ah!" Emi gasped.

"This…is bad, isn't it? Ms. Kisaki's one thing, but Chi, you know… Oh, no… We really screwed up."

"R-right, yeah. Chiho and her mother are probably back in Japan, too, besides—we just haven't seen them, is all. We really need to apologize to her parents…"

Now Maou and Emi were just as pale as the moment they lost Alas Ramus. Amane watched them, feeling a sort of pity.

This problem went beyond just exposing Chiho to danger multiple times. Maou and Emi, acting like sensible, decent people, had made a high school student engage in behavior that went well beyond the scope of regular life. That trip to Choshi where they met Amane was a particular issue, no doubt—Chiho's mom let her go because she believed Emi and Suzuno were sane members of society. Pretending Maou was just another dude, hiding his Devil King roots and letting

Chiho visit his apartment regularly (even if she wanted to)—that was far from commendable behavior, no matter how you sliced it.

"That and she fed me, she introduced me to MgRonald," Emi continued, "...and *look* at me..."

Maou owed a debt to Chiho's father as well; one he couldn't reveal to anybody. But he couldn't bring that up here.

"And we told a lot of lies about Alas Ramus, too," Emi said. "I can't count the number of times Chiho watched her for me. And I'm sure she told a lot of fibs to cover for that as well..."

"Funny to see the Hero and Devil King fretting over the same thing," Amane commented.

Neither of them were laughing. Then Amane decided to give the distressed couple even crueler news.

"Well, I'm sorry to spring this on you when you're worried about how dishonest you were with Chiho's mom, but we're not done talking yet. So about Alas Ramus..."

"...Huh?"

"Acieth's massive appetite, you know, and Alas Ramus mucking up the separation from your body...I think it's a sign that the Sephirah are about to go out of whack, the way Erone did before."

"Just a sign? Like it hasn't *really* happened yet?"

So eating sixty rice balls in a sitting wasn't going berserk enough? It was merely a sign of something yet to come?

"But it's not just because they've been separated from the world for so long, the way Erone was. It kind of has to do with what Chiho's doing right now. This was something Uncle George said, but..."

"Huh?"

Neither of them could fathom what Chiho had to do with the Sephirah breaking down.

"The Yesod, and also Malkuth, are particularly sensitive to the workings of mankind. They're represented by the astral and physical elements, too, so..."

"Um..."

"And then Ente Isla's Yesod shattered for whatever reason, and it created two beings—Alas Ramus and Acieth. I think what we have here are two people dividing up the burden that the full Yesod should be bearing. Which, you know, is fine. They both have their own circumstances and all…"

Amane paused. Given how freely she was speaking earlier, she now seemed oddly reluctant to continue.

"Right now, the top mission behind what Chiho's trying to do in Ente Isla is based on her not wanting to let you guys go. Now, as a side effect, that could lead to peace on that other world, and humans and demons bonding together across species and so on. But now Alas Ramus and Acieth are getting affected by it, and based on the role they play within Ente Isla's Sephirah, the vital elements involved with the human nature inside them are starting to come strongly to the surface. In the case of Acieth, that manifests itself in eating a lot."

""It's more than a lot.""

The two of them were growing adept at lashing back in chorus.

"Well, think about Acieth up to now. She's just a fragment, you know, and she's been stuck with Nord here in Japan for a really long time. If you picture this as something she's been storing up for years coming out all at once, it starts not seeming so strange."

"It's still pretty strange…"

"When you live in Japan, you know, you lose sight of just how hard it can be to keep your stomach full."

Amane flashed a triumphant smile.

"So, you know, Acieth we can handle. The real problem is Alas Ramus—for you guys, and for Chiho, too. Acieth's taking care of the part of the Yesod that's fulfilled by keeping her stomach full. But what's Alas Ramus responsible for? Well, based on her body and apparent age, I think it can make sense, but…"

With a grin that was conflicted if not quite strained, Amane looked at Emi.

"Have you guys not been able to give Alas Ramus much attention lately?"

"Huh? I…"

Emi was about say that wasn't true before stopping.

"You know…Bell and Eme and Alciel have been gone, so it's been hard to find much time to play with her. And my father's been focused on Acieth the whole time, too. So she's inside me the whole time I'm working…"

"What about the last time you went to Ente Isla?" Maou asked.

"We were all busy dealing with Kinanna, so I couldn't play with her much at all…"

"Well, Chiho's trying to bring peace to everyone in Ente Isla, and I think that's having a huge impact on Alas Ramus, you know? She's just a fragment, and she was alone for one heck of a long time, wasn't she? And now you guys are in the middle of all this uncertainty. I think that's a good way to stress out any young child."

"…All right," an impatient Maou said. "Level with me here. If Acieth's got a huge appetite, we can feed her and that solves it. But what're we gonna do about whatever's about to happen to Alas Ramus?"

"Well," Amane said, "brace yourself for this. A human, you know—especially a child—can't be kept starving for long. That's being literally personified with Acieth right now. So why do you think Alas Ramus is doing something to make Mommy and Daddy worry? Or *did* something, I should say?"

"Did something…? So separating out from me like that… Did she do that on purpose…?"

"She's seeking Mommy and Daddy's attention. She wants you to look at her more. She wants to feel all the overflowing love her parents can give her, no matter how much it is. That's why she's doing weird things like this."

"Ah…"

"And you two, Maou and Yusa, are the only people who can solve that problem. I hate to break it to Chiho and Kamazuki, but they're gonna have to step away."

Then, at that moment, Maou felt a dull foreboding deep inside his core. A sense that he was surrounded by issues he had no clue how to deal with, and now an even more sinister nightmare was careening toward him. Amane, meanwhile, just stared at them, looking almost sadistic.

"Maou... Yusa..."

The order she was about to give was like a death condemnation echoing from another world, a place that made hell seem like a pleasantly warm bath.

"You two need to live under the same roof."

"""......"""

The screaming that erupted from the man and woman in the room did nothing to disrupt the slumber of the Yesod sisters sleeping in the house.

※

"Chiho! You have a moment?"

"Uh-huh!"

Chiho looked up from her desk and turned around to face the caller at her door.

"Busy with more of that studying of yours?"

Visiting her, inside this chamber a good five times the size of her bedroom back home, was Dhin Dhem Wurs, a piece of parchment in her hand.

"You don't have to do that, ya know. You've stood up for yourself on the job here well enough, haven't you?"

"That's about as unrealistic as asking you to leave your job and enjoy retirement over in Japan."

Wurs, who was rating Chiho's talents about a hundred times greater than Chiho herself would, had been visiting her frequently during her stays in Ente Isla, trying every trick in the book to recruit her. Her inexhaustible obstinacy reminded Chiho of Sariel in many ways, but she had learned well how to sidestep her advances.

"You're going home tomorrow morning, ain't ya? I packed a souvenir along with your papers. Go enjoy them with your mother."

"Thank you very much."

The official Northern Island mission in the city of Noza Quartus was currently undergoing preparations for the upcoming international summit, a full legion of the Mountain Corps providing security.

"Were you returning to Phiyenci after this?"

"That's a lot to ask from *these* old bones. 'Course, I know I'm pushing a lot on you already…but I'm here for more than a cup o' tea with you today. I have some rather bizarre news for you."

"Bizarre…?"

"Bell was beside herself with it. She said there was an emergency over in Japan."

"You didn't read the letter?"

Chiho was staying here in the mission, with Wurs's blessings—but since Wurs was participating in the summit, Chiho had to treat her the same as everyone else involved.

"Nah, well, I had a look."

A questioning look emerged from Wurs's wrinkled face as she handed Chiho the letter.

"You know, I didn't think it was about anything in particular, really. Bell's part of the summit, too, so it's not like she could be in close contact with you, sort o' thing. And when I said Bell was beside herself, I just meant that's how her messenger seemed to me, y'know."

"Oh…"

Wurs was in no hurry to get her point across, but Chiho accepted the letter anyway.

"And this was written by Suzuno?"

"Well, the news was sent from someone in Japan, anyway, but… you know, if you ask me, is it really *that* worth letting you know about? That's what I say."

Since she'd begun visiting Ente Isla on the regular, Chiho had learned how to handle parchment paper like this, something she had a lot of exposure to here. She gave it a quick read, and:

"*Aaahhhhhhhhhhhh…*"

She let out a sigh, long and loud, like she was blowing away all the exhaustion built up over the past day.

"Amane...why did you do that...? And why is Suzuno in a panic about it at *this* point?"

"Hmm?"

"*Ahhh*... Now I don't want to go back tomorrow."

"But don't you have a lot to return to? Your school, and your 'prep center,' and your 'club sports' or whatnot?"

"I do, but... But I don't want to run into any of them and make them think I hurried back for *this* reason."

"Huh?"

"...But all right. At least I know Ente Isla's holding on to peace well enough that Amane can tell Suzuno about it without any huge problem. If barely."

"What would Bell be concerned about?"

"Allow me to keep that a secret...for the sake of her dignity. I don't think it's that devastating or anything, no. *Ahhh*..."

With another sigh, Chiho looked out the chamber window. Noza Quartus was a big city, but there were still dozens of times more stars in the sky than she'd ever see in Tokyo. They looked beautiful to her.

"I'm sure this is gonna freak everyone out a little, though... Hmm?"

Then something small, from the back of her mind, caught her attention.

"Under the same roof... Under the same roof... Together, together..."

"What is it, Chiho? You have a stomachache or something?"

Chiho smiled at the very grandmotherly concern, shaking her head. Then she exclaimed, "Stomach... Wait! That's it!"

"Hmm?"

"Listen, can I ask you a favor?"

As a rule, Dhin Dhem Wurs was extremely indulgent with Chiho. She accepted most of her requests, unless they were totally beyond the pale—and this request, too, was a piece of cake for her.

"...As long as we can get everything arranged—this is under the pretext of Noza Quartus hosting, of course, with me as an assistant—this could become rather interesting, yes!"

The proposal uncharacteristically surprised Wurs at first, but she quickly gave it a satisfied nod.

"All right. I'll talk matters over with Arvaim and try to get as much as I can for you."

"Thank you very much! If you're missing anything, I can buy it for you, so!"

"Of course! *Now* this is getting fun!"

THE DEVIL AND THE HERO LIVE UNDER THE SAME ROOF

One stop away from Meidaimae Station on the Keio Inokashira Line express train was Eifukucho Station, where one could step off and walk about five minutes to reach the Urban Heights Eifukucho apartments. This was the home of Emilia Justina, Hero of the Land of the Holy Cross—in effect, the headquarters of Ente Isla's savior.

Maou's mouth hung open. "W-wow..."

"..."

The sigh of wonder at the building's majesty made Emi all but grit her teeth.

"It's only two minutes' walk to a convenience store! I...I'm not *that* surprised by an autolock. I see 'em all the time in my deliveries... What do people even *use* the sofa here in the lobby for?! ...You've got *three* elevators?!"

"Would you shut *up* for a minute?!"

The honed shout from Emi made the person next to her quiet down with a shiver. Getting off at the fifth floor, she stood in front of the door deepest down the corridor, bracing herself as she put the key in the hole.

"Let me just say this," she said before turning it. "If you try to do anything funny in here—I don't care if it's in front of Alas Ramus or not—you're gonna be dead the very next second."

"Haven't heard you be all defensive like this in a while."

"Of course you haven't. Never in my *life* did I expect this to happen."

Resigned to her fate, Emi opened the door with a great lament:

"What horrible twist of fate would ever force me to invite the Devil King to my own home?!"

The sight that greeted Maou as he balanced a large backpack on his shoulders made his eyes flash wide.

"Damn, it's *huge*!"

The kitchen space itself, visible through the doorway, looked big enough to house the entirety of Room 201 of Villa Rosa Sasazuka. It featured a large sink, a roomy refrigerator, and—

"…Your slippers."

"Huh?"

"The slippers you bought on the way here. Put 'em on."

"Oh…"

There, by the door, were two pairs of slippers—one large, one small. Both looked pretty broken in.

"Wow, it's hard to get comfy in these…"

"No running around here in just socks, all right? If you do, I'm sending you down on hands and knees to wipe the floors."

Meekly obeying the pressure of the take-no-prisoners command, Maou took out the slippers he purchased along the way and put them on. He seemed uncomfortable in them.

As he minced into the apartment proper, Emi closed the door behind her with a resigned sigh. The air around them now fully belonged to the room's interior, bringing with it the "aroma" of the place.

"You know, it's kind of surprising, actually," Maou said.

"…What is?"

"Like, this is my very first time in your apartment."

"…Yeah. Not that you ever needed to be here."

"Well, thanks for letting me in. I know you're the boss around here, so I'll do what you say, okay?"

"…" Now Emi felt hesitant to lock the front door.

"Hey, aren't you gonna lock it? Whether or not you've got an autolocking front door, that's not very careful."

Maou, of course, failed to get the picture.

"...You're saying *that* to me?"

Emi twisted the lock hard, almost ripping it off as her face contorted.

"...Why does this have to happen...?"

Recalling the monumental events of three days ago, she couldn't help but sit down there by the front door, collecting herself.

✳

"Look, whether it'll help Alas Ramus or not, I absolutely cannot allow it. You need to give us some other method," Emi insisted.

"I'm not exactly a fan of it, either, but do you have to be *that* blunt about it?" Maou said.

"Ah-ha-ha-ha-ha!!"

Amane must have expected it all—Emi's flat refusal, Maou's sheepish rebuttal—because it almost made her fall off the sofa.

"Oh, you guys are the *best*! I heard you were getting along better these days so I figured you'd react a little more normally, but you should have seen the looks on your faces!"

"I'm not sure what kind of reaction you expected, but I can't do it. It's simply impossible." Emi sharply shook her head. "Why? Why would I ever be forced to live together with this man?"

"Your partner, you mean?"

"...He acts as Alas Ramus's dad. I'll recognize that. But I *refuse* to let you describe him as *that*."

"Wow! Man, it really *is* complicated between the two of you, isn't it?"

"Amane, are you poking fun at us? Because this is serious business involving Alas Ramus. I apologize for coming here and bothering you in the middle of the night, but I need you to be more serious with us."

"Ahhh-ha-ha-ha!!"

"Amane!!"

The more serious and composed Emi tried to be, the closer Amane came to bursting out in hysterical laughter.

"Ahhh, I'm sorry, I'm sorry. It's just so funny to me because it wasn't the reaction I expected at all. But…y'know, sorry to disappoint, but I *am* serious."

Amane repositioned herself in her seat, leaning forward a bit as she tried to soothe her captives.

"Maou, Yusa, and Alas Ramus. It needs to be the three of you living together."

"…How is that ethically feasible? 'Cause I mean, frankly, you're asking me to room with Emi, you know?" Maou wasn't being as coldly rigid with his choice of words, but he had zero interest in the concept, either.

"Please, even if it's just an idea, don't even describe it as 'rooming' with me. I don't want to hear that again if it kills me." Emi aimed the full brunt of her anger at Maou, all but ready to take Acieth's place in the food-driven death-ray department.

"Huh…?" Then Amane started wincing herself. "Why is a Devil King who staged a worldwide massacre talking to me about ethics?"

"Is that really worth discussing at the moment? That's not the point."

"Well, I mean, you still see people from really conservative families who swear they'll never do it, but it's…like, some people have hang-ups about living with someone they love before getting married, yeah? But you guys *hate* each other, so sharing a place wouldn't change much, would it?"

"Amane, do you realize how little sense you're making?" Maou asked.

"Because it's not about 'living' with him," Emi explained. "I don't want the Devil King to spend even a single second inside my home."

"Aww, but Yusa, you're going in and out of Maou's place all the time, aren't you?"

"It's completely normal for a Hero to storm an invasion of the

Devil King's lair! And it's completely unthinkable for the Devil King to visit the Hero's house!!"

"Hmm, maybe..."

Maou seemed convinced for a moment. But Amane just smirked at them, eyes turning positively evil.

"...Hee-hee-hee-hee-hee... Sounds like *you* just let the cat out of the bag, Yusa."

"H-how?!"

"I didn't specify *where* you'd be living, did I? So, Yusa, why are you assuming that I wanted y'all to live in your apartment, *hmmmm*?"

"...Oh." Maou looked at Emi, things now dawning in his mind. But Emi's face went even more neutral than before.

"I'm sure you're making fun of me," she flatly stated, "but Libicocco is living in Room 201 of Villa Rosa Sasazuka right now. I don't see how he fits into your happy-family scenario. And besides," she added with a grimace, "I'm sure I have a far more suitable environment for Alas Ramus at my apartment. If I bring all her clothing, her toys, her bath stuff, and her eating utensils to Devil's Castle, there won't be any free space on the floor to step on. I loathe the mere concept of this, but if you're picturing us living together, my address is the only option."

"Tssh... You're a lot colder than I thought, Yusa. Not gonna make this easy, huh? I figured you'd be beet-red and blowing your top right now."

"Amane..." It was hard to tell how serious Amane, queen of slippery talk, was being. It made Maou rub his head.

"But—and again, sorry—*but*," Amane went on, "this is really the only option that's gonna work. You don't want Alas Ramus spittin' laser beams like Acieth, right? Or turning all weird-looking and wrecking the city like Erone did?"

"...!"

Not even Emi could counter that. They were trying to help Alas Ramus, but if something happened and they couldn't deal with it, Emi knew she'd regret it.

"W-well, how about this, maybe? Bell's in Ente Isla right now, so maybe I could live in Room 202 for the time being? The Devil King will be right next door, and if you think of that building as a big house, I think that means we'd just be one room apart, but..." She knew she'd regret it, but Emi tried desperately to counter. "And my father's down on the first floor. Multigenerational families aren't that uncommon these days, right?"

"Stickin' to your guns, huh?"

Amane seemed a bit impressed at the struggle. She thought for a moment, crossing her arms.

"But ain't Libicocco still gonna be in the way? It's great if she has Mommy, Daddy, and Grandpa with her and all, but Daddy's coworker sharing a bedroom, too? That situation doesn't sound too feasible to me."

"But Alciel and Lucifer are close to Alas Ramus, and *they* work for the Devil King, too! And Bell's usually there all day as well! I think it boils down to the same thing!"

"Nah, if we're aiming for a 'happy family' kinda scenario here, I don't think we can have Ashiya or Urushihara or Kamazuki involved in the game, but..."

"Well, *we're* not connected to Alas Ramus by blood, either, but *we're* family to her! Libicocco ought to be just fine!"

"Hey, I'm not saying a family can't be structured like that, okay? But ethics or laws aren't the problem here—it's what Alas Ramus will accept. And maybe Alas Ramus accepts Ashiya and everyone else as family, but is Libicocco at that level?"

"Probably not. Not on the same level as Ashiya and Urushihara and Suzuno."

"Devil King! Can you defend us a little, please?! Don't you have any ideas? *You* don't wanna live with me, do you?!"

He didn't. But how to put it? Maou couldn't help but think that trying to disprove the structure of their family was running counter to the whole point of the debate. Besides, Maou never looked toward Emi with as hostile an eye as Emi did with him.

Whenever Alas Ramus got involved, Maou tended to go on the defensive.

"Well, I don't like the idea much, but if it's for Alas Ramus's sake..."

"Nnngh..."

And if that was Maou's stance, the way Emi was balancing her child against her own feelings made her feel like a failure as a parent. Working mothers were no longer uncommon in society; a woman was not necessarily expected to devote herself wholly to child-rearing at the expense of her career. Regardless, the first thought on any parent's mind needed to be their child's development—and removing that from your list of goals in life was never going to be looked upon favorably.

Right now, it was clearly Emi, not Maou, who was sticking to her guns and turning her eyes away from Alas Ramus's troubles.

"...That being said, there's something I want to make clear, too. First, like I've said many times before, Emi and I aren't married. We're not even lovers," Maou reminded them.

"Don't be crude..." Emi grimaced.

"So, you know, no matter how it looks to people around us, I think it's pretty clear that it'd be nothing like what some people want to imagine. So I'm okay with that aspect of it."

"Please, stop!" Emi was almost shouting.

"But I also have Acieth to think about," Maou continued. "The distance between Emi's place and Sasazuka is obviously farther than I can venture away from her. If I'm gonna live in her apartment, Acieth will have to join me. But right now, Acieth's still a hairbreadth away from going berserk, and we don't have the ability to feed her enough. I'm assuming you don't have a gas-powered, industrial-size rice cooker in your place, right, Emi?"

"Of, of course not!"

Emi was still in denial, but Maou, at least, was taking a constructive approach, addressing the disadvantage of this plan. It gave Amane a little bit of a surprise as she watched.

"That, and there's also Nord. We definitely need his permission for this, don't we?"

"...A mass-murdering demon is asking for the woman's father's permission?" Amane scoffed.

"Well, yeah, he's a victim of mine. We might have a decently neighborly kinda thing going on right now, but I'm sure he's not even close to forgiving me. There's no way he'd say yes to someone like me living with his daughter, is there? Even if the lines we're drawing are crystal clear. I'm willing to do anything for Alas Ramus, but you see how much Emi's against it and there are some real obstacles in the way of it, so I don't see how living in her place is realistic at all. Personally, I think her borrowing Suzuno's room for a while is our best choice, but—"

"...Devil King."

"..."

Maou's logical, reasonable argument made Amane's face turn somber. She sighed, then turned away from them, calling out the doorway.

"It's sounding pretty much like how we expected, but what do you think?"

"Huh?"

The door to the living room opened, revealing Nord on the other side.

"F-Father... You heard that...?"

"I will take care of Acieth for you. Please, don't hesitate to do what you have to for Alas Ramus."

He was carrying a tray stacked up with balls of rice—reinforcements for Acieth, no doubt. But then he left just as quickly as he came, turning around without another word.

"Father, wait!"

Emi ran after him, unsatisfied. She caught up in front of Acieth's bedroom, but he motioned for her to be quiet, confusing her.

"...Acieth is sleeping, I think. Emilia, look at this."

Looking inside the room, they saw Acieth sleeping peacefully, a calm smile on her face as she held hands with Alas Ramus.

"...!"

But Emi wasn't looking at Acieth. Her attention was focused

entirely on Alas Ramus, and what she saw stunned her into silence. The Alas Ramus Emi knew wasn't there. She was now grown.

Before, she hadn't even reached Acieth's hips when standing up—but now, sleeping together, she was about as tall as her sister's shoulders. Her arms and legs were longer now, befitting a child; she now looked like someone in their early elementary school years. Bizarrely, the yellow dress she had on previously had grown in size with her body.

Recovering from the shock, Emi finally noticed the soft, glowing light on Alas Ramus's forehead.

"Her fragment... It's glowing?"

"Acieth's has been glowing frequently lately, too," Nord said with a nervous smile, "whether she's hungry or not. It puts me on edge every time...but I certainly never expected this."

He offered a rice ball to Emi. Emi absentmindedly picked it up, removed the plastic wrap around it, and took a bite.

"...It's good."

"We paid four thousand yen for five kilograms of that rice."

"Whoa."

"Emilia, I'm sure you realize it, but... Well, with the body fusion and all, you might think we're deeply connected to them...but in reality, it's a fragile, fragile link."

"...Yeah."

Maou had claimed he and Acieth were inseparable a moment ago, but everyone involved knew this wasn't necessarily the case.

"You love Alas Ramus, don't you?" Nord continued. "But have you ever thought about just how much more time you'll be spending with her?"

"...No."

"Once that war is over, nobody knows what's going to happen to them. I don't know if we're deliberately not bringing it up, or we're relaxed about it because Ms. Shiba and her family seem to be...but once it's over, there's no guarantee at all this child will stay with you."

"Father..."

"...When you were six years old, you know, you were about that size."

There was no doubt that Alas Ramus's sudden growth surprised Nord. But there was something more than that in his affectionate eyes as he looked down at his "granddaughter" quietly sleeping.

"And that's what children do, Emilia. They grow. You may think they're so small, but you turn around one day and it's always, 'Good heavens, since when did she get like that?' You and the Devil King... Have you ever had one of those moments, looking at Alas Ramus?"

Children grow. It's an obvious fact, but just then, it sent Emi into a state of intense disorder.

"They grow... They grow..."

They were almost at exactly one year since Alas Ramus came to live with them. And yet...

"Emilia?"

"Father...I..."

As she stood there, about to cry despite herself, the words of Emi's father swept across her mind.

"Emilia, will you give some more open thought to living with the Devil King? Because, ever since long ago, back when Alas Ramus was separated from her Sephirah brothers and sisters...she hasn't had a chance to be part of 'one big family,' has she?"

"..."

It was in that moment that Emi relented.

"...Let me just note, that's really not something you should say to your unmarried daughter."

"Well, in another way, the two of you would put my mind at ease."

"Oh, don't start sounding like Amane with me... If Chiho or Bell or Eme find out, I don't even wanna *know* what they'll say..."

"I'm not too sure Chiho would say anything, would she?"

"That's what I'm afraid of! At least with Eme, she'd make it clear just how scared I should be of her. Ugghh..."

Finishing up the rice ball in her hand, Emi winced hard.

"And I understand if people want to picture the worst-case

scenario for how all this turns out. But what if...what if we have a *happy* ending? It's entirely possible, isn't it?"

"...Emilia?"

"You're right. It's still been a grand total of one day where she's lived together with both of her 'parents'—and even *that* was on the assumption Gabriel would take her the next day. But..."

Emi recalled the face of "Daddy," no doubt waiting and feeling helpless on the living-room sofa. She shook her head.

"But if everything turns out just fine, and Alas Ramus can keep hoping for happiness in the future... If it does...then I won't see myself as responsible for anything besides her, okay?"

As close as she seemed to crying, her face now had a resolved smile upon it.

*

And so Emi, Alas Ramus, and Maou agreed to live together in Room 501 of Urban Heights Eifukucho. The fact that this was an open-ended arrangement with no deadline unnerved her—but given that a whole week had passed and Acieth still hadn't settled down, it seemed natural that Alas Ramus would require at least that long herself.

"I wish Ignora and the heavens would just attack us instead of assassinating Archbishops or whatever. Then we could get this over with."

The thoughts on Emi's mind, as she cradled her head by the front door, were getting more and more agitated.

"Hey, Emi! Can I put my stuff wherever?"

"...One minute."

But this was reality. Maou had come to her home, and there was no undoing that. There were no obstacles between them now; she'd just have to find a way to survive each day.

For now, she advised Amane (who seemed to be in regular contact with Ashiya and the others) to inform the Ente Isla side of what was going on. With things being how they were, Emi didn't expect anyone to disagree with their choice, but deep down, she still had some faint hope that one of them would have an objection.

"Ahh..."

Resolving herself, she locked the security latch, put on her pair of slippers, and stepped into the apartment Maou had just infected with his presence.

"It's funny, though."

Maou had stepped into the living room inside, but was still waiting for her, keeping his backpack on his back.

"...What?"

She had noticed Maou was staring at all the walls, ceilings, and floors of the apartment. Anything she didn't want a man (Maou or not) to see, she had put away over the past three days, so there shouldn't have been anything too weird visible. Maou knew she lived in a big, condo-style apartment, so she figured he would have some comment about its size. She would be disappointed.

"You know, I have to say sorry to you."

"Huh?"

The apology, with a humble smile included, was so unexpected that Emi didn't know how to respond. What came next was even more unexpected.

"When you were asked to raise Alas Ramus out of nowhere by yourself...that must've been tough, huh?"

"Wh-what's *that* about?"

"No, I mean..."

Maou pointed at a chest of drawers in a corner of the living room. She had bought it when Alas Ramus began living with her; it was wooden, with four levels, but certainly nothing expensive. The bottom drawer was filled with bath towels for the girl, the second and third had assorted clothing, and the two half-sized drawers on the top were filled with socks on one side, washcloths and the like on the other.

"That's all stuff for Alas Ramus, right?"

"How did you know that?"

Among all the friends who'd visited her here, the only person who'd brought up that chest was Emeralda, who'd stayed for an extended period. It seemed doubtful that Emeralda ever told him about it...

"I mean, like, all the other furniture and stuff looks like it's where it belongs, but this kind of sticks out a lot. And Alas Ramus decorated it, didn't she? All those stickers on the side..."

"Oh..."

Fair enough. The chest was laden with cute, colorful stickers. And this wasn't even all of them—the very first set had been repeatedly applied and reapplied, and by now they were probably working on layer number three. The crashing waves of stickers had even spread over to the shelving on top of the chest, used to hold things like wet wipes and moisturizing lotion.

Her silence prompted Maou to give her a few words of encouragement. "When she was living at my place, you know, she didn't have enough stuff to fill a dresser this size. It just made me think, like, you've been doing a lot for her."

"............Yeah." His words unnerved her. "Well, back then, you barely had enough things to clothe yourselves with, didn't you? Of *course* I would've given her some new stuff. But if you're gonna live here, you might as well learn about what's in there, so..."

"All right. I'll do that."

Emi meant to sound stern with him, but Maou just meekly nodded back.

"...Anyway, just put your stuff down somewhere and have a seat," she said. "I'll make someplace for your laundry later."

"All right. Thanks."

Maou looked around a little, then sat down on the wooden floor, deliberately avoiding the rug placed over it.

"...What are you doing?"

"Oh, I just thought you'd get angry if I sat on the sofa or carpet without asking."

"..."

Maou must have been trying to be considerate. Not even Emi was going to snap at him for something like sitting on her sofa—but she *had* done things like that to him in the past, she knew. It made for tough going now. In a way, Maou was being *too* careful, like a boy going into a girl's bedroom. Ever since the talk with Amane that led to this arrangement, Emi felt like she was being constantly reminded of how petty she was acting. It made this incredibly stressful for her, even though Maou had only been here about five minutes so far.

"Ugghh…"

With a soft groan, she opened the sliding door between the living room and the apartment beyond. She quickly looked over the other side, making sure everything was okay for Maou to look at, then focused herself.

"…Good."

The next moment, Alas Ramus—in her more familiar body size—was sleeping peacefully on the bed, bathed in a soft light. Relieved the process had worked as intended, Emi braced herself, feeling the eyes of the somewhat uncomposed Maou behind her.

"…Stand up a sec. I'll show you around."

"O-okay."

He had just been asked to sit down, but Maou didn't seem concerned. He came to his feet, walking up behind Emi.

"Let's start with the kitchen, I suppose. Here's the microwave; there's the refrigerator. The burners are up there. This is a normal faucet; this one's got a purifier attached to it. If you're drinking from the tap, use the normal faucet so the filter doesn't wear out so fast."

"Right. Okay."

She had spoken so fast that Maou readily nodded at her orders about the faucet without blinking. Again, she began to feel like she was being needlessly petty—and that feeling added to the stress.

"…But if you need hot water, you can fill the D-Far pot over there with filtered water if you like."

"Um…all right."

Maou sounded oddly hesitant to her. This was a much fancier, more complex kitchen than what Devil's Castle featured; maybe he wasn't up to speed on all the appliances on offer.

"Also, I cleared out the second shelf up in the refrigerator for your use, so if you bring in takeout or buy something you don't want me to eat, put it in there."

"Oh, are you sure?"

Maou's eyes opened wide with surprise.

"...If you're asking me whether I'm sure you can use the refrigerator, well, if you want to get sick eating room-temperature food, then fine by me, but don't expect me to nurse you back to health. If you're surprised that I'm giving you your own space, well, I've kept this shelf free for guests ever since Eme crashed in here. It's gonna be annoying if you ask permission to use the refrigerator all the time, you know? Even *I* have a conscience."

"Oh… Oh. Well, I'll use it, then. Can I put the water bottle I just bought in there?"

"…Go right ahead."

Like a new part-time hire who felt completely out of place, Maou took a few self-conscious steps into the kitchen, removing a half-liter plastic bottle from his bag and placing it on its side in the fridge's second shelf.

"But we can share the milk, okay? There's not enough space for two of them. But keep in mind, Alas Ramus is watching, so don't drink it from the carton or anything like that. If you use a lot or it's just about out, let me know—and I'll do the same for you. All right?"

"A-all right."

Maou solemnly nodded. There was now a pen and paper in his hands.

"As for ice, there's a tank in the fridge you can fill water with, so if we're running short, go ahead and make some more."

"Huh? The tank's in the fridge, not the freezer? So where's the ice?"

The moment she heard the question, Emi could accurately predict her future five seconds from now.

"…The water flows down from here, and then the ice comes out here."

She opened the drawer that contained the finished ice.

"Whooaaaaa…"

Maou stared at the ice, mouth agape—exactly as Emi imagined he would, five seconds previous.

"Ugh…"

With a sigh, she closed the refrigerator.

"…So here's where I keep the dishes and things."

"Right."

"Except for emergencies, I'll be doing all the cooking, so you won't need to touch the cooking utensils. Just remember that Alas Ramus's dinnerware is in here. I'll want you to buy some glasses, rice bowls, chopsticks, and silverware for yourself later. For today, you can just use my disposable plates and chopsticks."

"This reminds me of all the lectures you used to give me."

"Do you want to die?"

It was kind of a trip back in time for Emi as well. At the same time, she resolved to quit bantering with Maou any further, lest her murderous rage be stoked any more than it already was.

"Let's go to the washbasin and the bathtub. First, lemme make it clear…"

Just as Emi was giving Maou a particularly sharp look, a voice called out, "Mommy…? I'm hungry…"

"Oh?"

"Hmm?"

A small figure unsteadily walked up to them.

"Alas Ramus, you're awake?" Emi asked.

"Mmm, I'm hungry…"

She wobbled up to Emi's legs, grabbing one of them around the knee. Then she looked up. A smile came across her face.

"Daddy's here!!"

"Y-yeah, I sure am!"

"Huh? I… Daddy? Wow! Daddy!"

She seemed confused at this unprecedented event—but once she was sure this was Emi's apartment and he was really inside of it, she promptly grabbed his hand.

"Daddy! Daddy! Let's play!!"

"Oh, um, sure, Alas Ramus. Calm down, okay? I'm busy learning about some things from Mommy right now..."

"No! I wanna play!"

"Whoa, whoa..."

Pulled by the unusually excited Alas Ramus, Maou was taken to a corner of the living room.

"Daddy! Look!"

There, next to the TV stand, was a yellow cloth-covered box. Alas Ramus whipped the lid open, then tilted it over, spreading the contents all over the floor.

"Ohh?"

"Alas Ramus! I keep *telling* you not to empty the box out like that!"

It was full of a diverse range of toys—some large, some small; some featuring characters Maou knew, others with weird designs he had never seen; some cheap-looking, others fancier. They comprised Alas Ramus's personal treasure trove, and now they were all scattered across the carpet.

"Daddy! Wanna eat curry?"

"Huh? Curry?"

Among the toys was a pretend-cooking set.

"Well, um, sure, can I have some?"

"Okeh! Comin' right up!"

Maou turned toward Emi for a moment. She didn't move, simply watching them from the kitchen. Having no other recourse, he waited for Alas Ramus to somehow produce curry from the mountain of toys she had.

"Okeh, here you go!"

He was rewarded with a plastic saucepan containing a mountain of plastic fruit slices, stuck inside with Velcro, with a fork and the tail of a fish sticking out.

"Umm..."

"It's melon-and-fish curry!"

"Ohhh. Okay..."

He gave Emi another distressed look. She listlessly stared back at him, as if testing him.

"Ah...um..."

"Enjoy!" Alas Ramus said proudly.

Maou gingerly took the melon-and-fish curry, then used the round plastic fork to pretend to eat it. "Ooh, it's really tasty!"

"You can't eat it yet!"

"Huh?!"

With a smile, the chef took the melon-and-fish curry from his hands and gave him a toy teacup in its place.

"Tea first!"

"Oh, thanks..."

"Is it gooooood?"

"Y-yeah?"

"Good how?"

"Hmm? How? Umm... Well, it's nice and sweet, I think?"

"Nah-uh!"

"Huh?"

Alas Ramus never engaged in this kind of make-believe play back in Room 201. Now Maou felt like the one being toyed with.

"Ah, um, can I have that curry now?"

"Sorry! Curry's sold out!"

"Oh, come on!"

The melon-and-fish curry must've been scarfed down by someone else in the meantime. Maou couldn't help but laugh.

"Daddy, look!"

The next moment, she was clutching something else in her hands, the tea and curry now gone as she thrust it in front of Maou.

"Alas Ramus, is that...?"

"Happi'ess Set!"

Maou knew what it was. It was a toy meant for little girls, given away around half a year ago with the Happiness Sets they sold for kids at MgRonald. Some tie-in with the Relax-a-Bear company, presumably.

"This is your thing, isn't it?" he asked Emi, knowing she was a fan of that franchise. The question finally brought her to life.

"It's really well-made, actually," Emi said. "And whatever I like, Alas Ramus generally likes, too, so..."

She approached them, sitting down next to Maou and making eye contact with Alas Ramus.

"Hey, Alas Ramus? Can you be a good girl and wait for just one second? Mommy has something important to talk about with Daddy."

"Somethin' important?"

"That's right. Daddy's going to be staying here for a little while, so I'm showing him how everything works around here."

"H-hey…"

Emi was using vocabulary she figured Alas Ramus would be able to grasp…but if she was coming out and saying it now, the child's reaction could very well dictate how the future would go. He knew Emi was aware of that—but if she was, she didn't betray it on her face at all. All this looked like was Emi treating Alas Ramus the way she always did, right in front of Maou.

Then:

"Daddy!!"

Alas Ramus beamed. Her face lit up as she shot to her feet, abandoning the mess of toys behind her, and grabbed Maou by the hand.

"Daddy! Daddy! This's the kitchin! The water comes out here!"

"…Uh-huh."

"And up there is the dishes! Rewax-a-Beaw glass!"

"…Ooh, really?"

"Uh-huh! And the fridge has yogurt! I can eat yogurt!"

"Right, right."

"And, and there's animal cookies here, an' I can't eat them unless Mommy says so…"

After touring the kitchen once with Mommy, Maou was now getting the rundown from her daughter's point of view. He smiled broadly. Emi didn't respond, instead silently putting away the toys on the floor that'd hurt if someone stepped on them.

This went on for a little while, Alas Ramus alternating between giving Maou a tour of the place and playing with him. By the time it occurred to Maou to look at his phone screen, it was already past four in the afternoon, with Emi busy rinsing the rice for dinner.

"Ah, Emi, what about dinner…?"

"Just go ahead and play with Alas Ramus, okay?"

"No, but, I don't have any dishes or chopsticks yet…"

"I was just messing with you. You can buy some if you want, but I've got enough spares and guest sets for you to use."

She didn't lift her face from her dinner prep as she spoke. And when she fell silent, Maou quickly had another job on his hands—the reading of five storybooks in a row, produced by Alas Ramus from parts unknown.

After a while, dinner was ready.

"…"

Maou was at the table with Emi and Alas Ramus. Like at his own place, there wasn't a dedicated dining table, just a low table on the rug in the living room that served as the center of activity around the apartment.

"I don't have another placemat for you, so let's go buy whatever else you need tomorrow."

In what was a small surprise to Maou, Emi and Alas Ramus both used placemats when eating. He knew what they were, of course, but he didn't think they were part of everyday family life, so it astonished him to see that Emi expected him to use one, too.

"Oh, um, I don't need a mat or anything…"

He began to deny it, since it wasn't an absolutely necessary part of tableware, but Emi was unexpectedly adamant.

"It's nothing expensive. Just think of it as for Alas Ramus's sake, okay? I had Eme use one, too—but she'll yell at me if I let you use hers, so…"

"…All right."

Despite her earlier jokes about paper plates and cups, Emi was much more insistent about *placemats*, of all things. It made no sense to Maou. She never even mentioned them when she joined the gang at Villa Rosa Sasazuka for dinner—maybe it was just her personal preference when dining at home. She was the boss around here, so Maou resolved to take a when-in-Rome approach.

A small spread of food was now steaming on the table, all in appropriate, non-paper tableware. There was white rice, miso soup with fried tofu and spinach, a big bowl of salad, some *shumai* dumplings from the grocery store...and the yogurt that was Alas Ramus's big thing as of late.

"Here, Alas Ramus."

"Okeh, thank you!"

"You're welcome... Devil King?"

"Huh? Oh... Right. Thanks for making dinner."

"Good job, Daddy!"

"...Thanks."

Maou, unsure what he should be doing, picked up his bowl of miso soup and took a sip.

"Ah..."

"What?"

"No, um, I bet you put a lot of sweat into this."

"What do you mean?"

Maou vaguely brushed off the topic. He meant to say that perhaps Emi, nervous to have him here, had broken out in a cold sweat that added to the soup's saltiness. Explaining the joke would just get him yelled at, though, so he didn't.

Then something more noteworthy came to mind.

"You know, come to think of it, isn't this the first time I've eaten your food?" he asked.

"..." Emi pondered this for a moment. "I thought for a second you were right," she said, sounding perfectly comfortable. "But looking back, I've brought along some homemade dishes to your place sometimes. Nowhere near as often as Chiho, but..."

"Oh, did you...? Hmm... Didn't you make a side dish out of *okara* tofu dregs once? You said there was this really good tofu place near you, I remember. Where was that place, anyway?"

"I'll tell you tomorrow. But also, during my MgRonald training, you tasted the fries and desserts and stuff I made, didn't you?"

"That doesn't really count."

And so things began to proceed much as they did over at Villa Rosa Sasazuka in normal times—occasionally chatting, occasionally

catering to Alas Ramus's needs, but overall letting the time fly as they enjoyed their dinner.

※

The moment Chiho returned from Ente Isla, her mother, Riho, opened her bedroom door and peeked inside.

"Oh, Chiho, you're back?"

"Hi, Mom."

"I saw your room light on, so I figured."

From this, it was pretty clear to tell that Riho had grown used to Chiho's behavior, not to mention events on Ente Isla.

"Have you eaten yet?"

"No. I've been busy, so I was doing my prep school homework."

"Ah. Are you going there now? Want me to whip up something real quick?"

"That'd be great, thanks."

"Don't overwork yourself, okay?"

"Well, I'm eating so well every day, I need to get *some* exercise, you know? Otherwise I'll be in trouble."

Dhin Dhem Wurs was giving her more meals and snacks at Noza Quartus than she could ever work off, so her weight had gone up a bit recently.

Over the last little while, she had developed a taste for Ente Islan cuisine, figuring out her favorites and so on, but her mother's home cooking always put her mind at ease. Swiftly taking in some rice, miso soup, and a quick omelet roll with *kombu* kelp, she found that even this snack relaxed her enough to begin feeling drowsy.

"Thanks a lot!"

"You can leave everything there. You need to get ready, right?"

"Yeah. I have most of it done—it really *is* a good idea to build a timetable in advance, huh? I'll see you later."

"Right, right, have a good time."

She had just gotten back from another world, and now she was hurriedly rushing away into the early evening. Watching her go,

Riho recalled the time not long ago when she'd first learned her daughter's secret.

To someone like Riho—who had left Japan only once on a school trip and didn't know much about lands and cultures outside her home nation—standing atop that hill overlooking the Northern Island capital of Phiyenci was beyond chaotic for her. She barely remembered it, in fact, not really calming down until the young man called Gabriel took her over to the so-called "Devil's Castle."

"...Mr. Maou certainly managed to build a...large place for himself," Riho remarked.

"*Bah-ha-ha-ha-haaa!!*" Gabriel laughed.

"Mom!"

That was Riho's reflexive reaction after being told this was Maou's true base of operations. It made Gabriel instantly crack up and Chiho give her a blushing, embarrassed look, much of the reason Riho remembered it so well.

Looking around the area, Riho saw crowds of people, none of them appearing Japanese. Seeing them made her realize just how higher up the totem pole Ashiya and Urushihara were...and also, despite not even noticing them at first despite their size, she discovered huge, nonhuman *creatures* mixed in with them all, some many times large than any normal person.

"Chiho?"

"...Yes, Mom?"

"...Do you remember when I took you to Hokkaido when you were young? The hills around Biei?"

"Huh?"

"I remember imagining these vast fields of flowers and things, like the pictures in the magazines. Then we went over, and it wound up being the worst rainstorm in years up there, right?"

"Oh, yeah, I remember."

"So we changed our plans and stayed one more night, and of course all the gardens and things were waterlogged, but it was still pretty in its own weird kind of way, I remember. That's what this view reminds me of."

"I...don't really get it."

"No? Well, I know this is an amazing sight—that I'm having this wondrous experience. But part of me is also...you know, 'this is it, huh?'"

"Mom?"

"This castle really *is* a surprise to me...but when I think how, well, of *course* you'd find it on a planet like this, then, you know... 'Wow, neat,' is about all I can think."

Chiho didn't seem to understand, but those were Riho's honest feelings.

Suddenly, Chiho turned around, detecting a Gate about to open at the base of Devil's Castle.

"Is that some kind of warp magic?"

"Yeah, pretty much...but I'm worried Yusa or Maou is coming over here to yell at me."

A trace of anxiety was present on Chiho's face.

It was true that neither Maou nor Emi seemed to comprehend what was going on the whole time during that MgRonald visit. If everything happening in Ente Isla was supposed to be a vital secret, Chiho couldn't blame them for being at least a little angry.

Instead, what appeared from the Gate was a woman whose clothing looked very familiar to Riho in a way, although she didn't recognize the face.

"Huh? Ms. Suzuki?!"

Chiho seemed to know the woman. She waved broadly toward her.

"Boy, I was *shocked* when I heard the story! You really took the plunge, didn't ya?"

"Hee-hee-hee..."

This was Japanese being spoken, a language that nobody here besides Ashiya, Urushihara, and Gabriel had ever heard before. Riho logically concluded that this "Suzuki" couldn't have just been a local with a Japanese-sounding name.

"Oh, are you Chiho's mother?"

"Y-yes, I am, um…"

"My name is Rika Suzuki. I'm Chiho's companion here…and yours, too, I suppose."

"…Of course. And my name's Riho Sasaki. Um, by 'companion,' do you mean…?"

"Well, in terms of getting caught up in Ente Isla stuff and having my life changed by it. Oh, and by the way, I can't cast magic or anything. I'm a hundred percent made in Japan! Kobe, to be exact."

"Oh…" Riho nodded at the pleasantly befitting turn of phrase. "So why are you here at Devil's Castle, Ms. Suzuki?"

"Ah, well, Chiho and Suzuno have been up to some pretty crazy stuff, and we figured you might be confused about a lot of things. So Ashiya asked me to help take care of you."

"Oh, well, um… Sorry to get you involved, I suppose…"

"It's all right! It gave me a chance to yell at Ashiya about how we're supposed to not be traveling and sending messages to each other and stuff."

"Aw, Ms. Suzuki…"

"So, yeah, I heard most of the story. And Chiho?"

"…Yes?"

"If I ever lose my job, can you introduce me to a decent one? Here in Ente Isla, maybe?"

"Aren't you supposed to be offering me encouragement or something?!"

"I heard from Ashiya," Rika said, "about most of what you're trying to do, Chiho. I'm in no position to act like I'm superior to you. It's about time for *me* to start seriously contemplating my life, too, so I'd love a chance to latch on to you and hopefully reap some of the profits!"

"Ms. Suzuki!"

"…"

"Okay, maybe I'm half-joking. But I can't really think of a future that doesn't involve this place in some way, so I wanna support you, Chiho. I heard the managers at MgRonald found out about you, but

I'm not gonna give up my position as your 'first friend' you let in on this, okay?"

"Ms. Suzuki…"

"…Ms. Sasaki, I'm sure a lot of this still seems unbelievable. If I just tell you everything out of nowhere, you'd probably be like 'who's this girl, coming in through a portal and giving me all this nonsense' and stuff. But everyone here is real nice people, y'know? And Chiho stands head and shoulders above all of them. It's not that she was hiding a secret from you so much as, you know, *carrying* it."

"…Well," Riho replied, "that's kind of the problem."

"Huh?"

"Mom?"

"…It really doesn't matter if Chiho had a secret or not. But as her mother, the fact that my daughter's in this vast other world, attracting the attention of all kinds of villains like it's her personal talent… and the fact that I never detected or even noticed it at all… That's the biggest problem."

She smiled, having few other options.

"By the way, Chiho, I was wondering… There wasn't a mountain over there earlier, was there?"

"Oh, that? Well, Kinanna's kind of got dementia, so I think he's sleeping after going on one of his tirades."

"………Here, Ms. Sasaki, why don't we just go home? I'm a normal human being, just like you, so…"

"…Y-yes. Um, but I think there's somewhere else I need to be taken first, so can you wait a little bit?"

Riho still wasn't sure why Rika Suzuki seemed in so much of a panic back then. But she figured asking wouldn't help her understand, and she was sure it was better not to ask anyway.

Quickly changing clothes and picking up the bag she used for prep school, Chiho pedaled her bicycle (one she'd barely used since entering high school) and set off. After she did, Riho closed the front door behind her.

"Hmm… You know, Ms. Takenouchi across the street told me about how empty it seemed around the house when the last of her children left…but now *I'm* starting to feel that way. Maybe I should have my husband take some time off and we can all go on a trip or something. Ohh, but how am I gonna explain *this* to him…?"

※

"Why are you contacting me at a time like this? You know how delicate your position is."

"…I fear I am descending into a state of self-loathing."

"What?"

The scene was Ea Quartus, an administrative city on the eastern edge of the Central Continent. Efzahan held formidable influence over this region, and it was here that Suzuno and Ashiya opted to meet.

"Has Amane been in contact with you, Alciel?"

"Amane? No. She may be visiting Urushihara over at Devil's Castle, but I have been traveling between here, Noza Quartus, and Devil's Castle frequently as of late for summit preparations, and he mentioned nothing in particular to me… Did something happen?"

"Yes, well…something…"

"If you have *that* haggard of a look on your face, there must be an issue with Emilia or Alas Ramus, no? I thought Acieth was in a state of semi-remission."

"Well, um, you see, they have all been up to a few things…"

"You are being vague. But how are negotiations going with Cervantes Reberiz and the other Archbishops? Well, I hope? Because controlling Cervantes *should* be job one for you right now."

"I know. With that, there are no problems to speak of. Lord Cervantes is a shrewd man, aware of his own interests. Someone who must not be antagonized, but given his nature, once you take care of the vital points, he is easier to wrangle than the other two. So…yes, all is well, but…"

Suzuno chose her words carefully.

"Amane delivered the news to me first, I believe. I thought I should tell you and Chiho, and I heard you were in Ea Quartus, so…"

"I must meet with the Orange Scarves' commander soon. Please keep it brief…"

"Did you hear about the Devil King's plans to stay in Emilia's home?"

"I shall postpone my meeting. Let me hear you out."

Ashiya was barely paying attention to Suzuno before. Now, suddenly, he looked straight at her.

"Did something serious happen to Alas Ramus?"

He had a cool enough head to reach that conclusion instantly. But as cool as his head was, there was a grim light to his eyes.

"Well, it would seem so, yes. It was decided that the Devil King and Emilia living together would be the best solution, so, well, they are aiming to create a normal, loving family environment for her, and…"

"I see. And this is not a case of the Devil King finding unpaid debt or some other dirt about Emilia and exploiting it against her will?"

"I think you would know by now that Emilia is not the type to have such things in her background."

"That is not what I am asking. I trust that this is His Demonic Highness's decision, but if he's decided to take residence in Emilia's home, there must be monumental events driving his resolve. If you are flying over here so urgently to inform me, I feared at first that some calamity had befallen Japan. But given how my liege has bent over backward many times before for Alas Ramus's sake, I hardly see any reason for surprise."

Some slight sense of relief seemed to prevail in Ashiya's mind. But he still eyed Suzuno with abject suspicion.

"Or should I take this to mean you believe my liege and Emilia are operating under some misunderstanding, or other nefarious circumstance?"

"…No, honestly, I do not see that as the case at all. At *all*. Now I am starting to wonder whether it was immature of me, being agitated enough to inform Chiho with such haste."

"Well, judging by her behavior the other day, I hardly think something like the Devil King and Emilia living together would faze her."

Ashiya himself was involved in Chiho's big reveal, behind the scenes. He had kept track of her moves afterward, both with his own eyes and through other people. He had always seen her as a unique young woman, but over the past few days of summit preparations, she had handled the dignitaries of Noza Quartus and the Northern Island without getting overwhelmed. He understood that she was juggling this with school, club activities, and her exam-prep academy. It truly astonished him.

That was why he found it so befuddling that Suzuno—a woman at the head of the Church, someone with far more life experience than Chiho—was acting so impulsive, like a person who'd had too much to drink.

"Of course," he said, assuming a more conciliatory tone, "the issue with the assailant in the space suit remains unsolved, but Emilia—Alas Ramus included—remains a vital part of our arsenal. If an issue has occurred with Alas Ramus, I can certainly understand why you'd like me to know."

"Along those lines, I think we will not have to worry about a cataclysmic event along the lines of Erone's and Acieth's. Apparently, when Emilia tried to manifest Alas Ramus from her body, she reappeared a great distance from her, next to Acieth…"

She was still sounding vague, but she relayed the information Ashiya needed to know.

"Well, that is all fine and good while she remains in Japan…but it *is* a problem, yes. If she should reappear in the wrong place, she could be captured or wrested away from us, no?"

"Yes. And that is why, I think, they are taking measures to prevent matters from getting worse. Um, how to put it…?"

"Hmm?"

"…Never mind."

"You are acting rather elusive. What is the matter?"

It was a simple question, and it still visibly fazed her.

Suzuno knew she was acting strangely. But she also felt that revealing...*that* to Ashiya didn't quite seem right. She had been discussing her feelings for Maou in ways that ventured well into TMI territory by Japanese standards—but, so far, only to other women she was close to. If she revealed it to Ashiya as well, she could very well be eyed with an enigmatic sort of hostility in many ways. It'd open her to criticism for focusing on the wrong things at the wrong time.

"...Well, to be honest, I have an audience with the head of the Inlain Azure Scarves shortly, as part of my mission from Lord Cesar. However, all the clerics accompanying me work for Lord Cesar, and it's proving quite annoying to deal with them..."

"That sounds like a needless distraction to me. Remember, no matter what happens, we are working strictly in a world of human beings."

He was right. But regardless, Suzuno had just barely saved herself from broaching a dangerous topic.

Leaving the office chamber Ashiya occupied, Suzuno—who was telling the truth about Cesar's mission—prepared to go back to negotiating between Cesar's Crusade frontline forces and the Eight Scarves' Central Continent force leaders.

"...Archbishop Crestia, if I may..."

"What is it?"

She still wasn't used to being called "Archbishop," but after several days of this, she was finally answering to it without hesitation. She had undergone the (somewhat abbreviated) purification ritual, so everyone nearby was treating her like an Archbishop, whether the official ceremony had taken place or not.

"A messenger from Saint Aile made contact with us earlier."

"A messenger? For me? Is it from Director Emeralda?"

If anyone needed to contact her right now, it was Emeralda. Surprisingly, though, the message was from Rumack.

"General Rumack is in Ea Quartus on business as well, and

apparently she's carrying some problems from her home nation that she wants you to preside over."

"What? I'm hardly going to hold confessionals out here."

That sounded ominous to Suzuno—as enigmatic as it was nebulous. Maybe Rumack just wanted to reach out to her, but she was a member of the upcoming summit, too. Contacting Suzuno in public was something she ought to be avoiding.

"...Tell her that we could meet this evening, but only in an unofficial capacity."

"Yes, Archbishop."

Distractions like these were best handled quickly. Suzuno wanted any potential sparks thoroughly stamped out before they got any closer to the day of the summit. But when night came and Rumack visited her guarded hotel room in Ea Quartus, Suzuno was taken aback by how clearly hostile she looked.

"General Rumack?"

"Good evening, Archbishop Crestia."

"...Are you angry that I didn't tell you about my ordination, or about my background?"

Rumack and Suzuno were personally acquainted via their relationships with the Devil King's Army, but calling them "friends" would be a stretch. Both of them were the type who couldn't abandon any cause or mission they'd taken up. Considering her public activities, if Rumack was mad at Suzuno, it likely had to do with her Archbishop ordination, and how Rumack and Emerada's interference with the Crusade wound up having the opposite effect intended as a result.

Now, however, with Cervantes officially part of the summit, Suzuno didn't see how it was that much of a problem. So she put on her "public figure" mask as she dealt with Rumack.

"Understand that I was not hiding my birthplace. This ordination came as a surprise to me as well, so—"

Rumack stopped her argument midway.

"What I'd...wish...to say about that *does* matter, but for the moment it can be set aside. The reason I'm angry, Crestia, is because of how carelessly you're acting."

"Hmm? Carelessly how?"

Suzuno raised an eyebrow. She had been going around the northeastern part of the Central Continent lately, and she couldn't think of anything on her itinerary that affected Rumack at all. But the next moment, her heart almost leaped out of her.

"Is it true that Emilia and the Devil King have begun living together?"

"*Whaaa?!*"

She could almost see her heart literally escaping her lips, beating in the air ahead of her. It made her blink helplessly several times. Why would *that* ever come out of Rumack's mouth? But the next moment, Suzuno feared all her other organs were going to be ejected out of her as well.

"And is it true the direct cause of this was *your* love confession to him?"

"No, no, no, no, no, no, no, no, General Rumack, what are you saying, it is absolutely untrue, *absolutely* untrue, there must have been some crossed wires, why, is *that* what you heard?!"

"We have reliable information that Archbishop Crestia has dedicated her heart and soul to the Devil King, but…?"

"Who could *ever* say such an insane, irresponsible thing?!!"

The sentry standing guard outside knocked on the door, hearing the commotion. "Wh-what is the matter?!" he asked, rushing in.

"Nothing! Back to your post!"

Suzuno blocked him with supersonic speed and force, and then:

"Ge-Ge-Gen-General Rumack, we must put our information together. What you've been told is preposterous in many ways. I think we should go through every piece of it."

"Fine. I'd like to know the truth as well, if I could. Emeralda, you realize, is wholly impossible to deal with right now, as angry as she is. Between this and the whole affair with the Crusade supply route, she even threatened to send an assassin to your ordination to do away with you for good."

"Ah...ugghhh... Why is this happening...?"

"That's what I'd like to know. Because I don't know what's going on over there, but I'll have you know that the Emperor, the crown prince, our congress, our government administrators, even the royal guard—I gotta keep my eyes on *all* of them, and none of them actually know what's going on. And instead of that, I have to go on this ri-*dic*-ulous errand for them instead."

Rumack spat out the words, sincerely peeved about it all. Suzuno felt the need to be careful with hers.

"...General Rumack, were you sent all the way to Ea Quartus just to ask me the truth about that?"

"If I was, Saint Aile and I would leave the summit. I have an audience planned with the Azure Emperor as well, more or less."

Treating a meeting with the man who ruled over a quarter of the world as a side project probably indicated just how much rage Emeralda had directed toward Rumack about this subject.

"Ugh... Well, to avoid any future misunderstandings, it would seem that the Devil King and Emilia have been forced by events to share a living space. It is related to the Sephirah going out of control, and it is a vital part of preparing for the war against heaven."

"Emeralda understands all that. She's *still* flying into a rage."

"I cannot take responsibility for that," Suzuno replied with a sigh.

"...Look," Rumack continued, "I, too, have interacted personally with both Emilia and the Devil King. Yes, it surprised me how little strife there is between the two of them...but I would not call their relationship particularly friendly, either."

"Right?! That is precisely right! And I heard how the Devil King and Emilia were both dead set against it, but were faced with no other choice!"

"Yes, but the way Emeralda puts it...as dry as their relationship may seem right now, all it takes is a single unexpected spark to set it aflame..."

"That's *none* of my business!!"

Now they were actively squabbling with each other. Through Rumack, though, one thing was now clear: Emeralda would never accept Maou and Emi under one roof in a million years. By the time she showed up here, she might even start blaming Suzuno for the two of them seeing Alas Ramus as "their" daughter.

"So, what of the story about you, a Church Archbishop, inveigling with the King of Demons?"

"General Rumack! You're enjoying every moment of this, aren't you?!"

"If I didn't, how would I ever will myself to be here?"

Rumack threw her whole body across the sofa.

"Look, I really don't care who's fancying someone, or falling for someone, or duking it out with someone. Frankly, I know I'm on a level below the other summit participants. I have an Emperor above me, which means I wield less power than the heads of state I'll be with. I don't have the heroic reputation of someone like Emeralda—essentially, I'm between a rock and a hard place. Now, if all of us here were secretly striving for peace, that would inspire me to try a little harder…but instead, everyone's going on about couples, and trysts, and other romantic entanglements! Alciel, Lucifer, and Albert are the only ones making any kind of effort! You know? Aren't you ashamed of yourself, letting the men show you up like this?"

"General Rumack…"

"Maybe I should do away with the Devil King, push Alciel as his successor, then invade the damn world myself!"

"General Rumack! We don't know who might be listening!"

"Oh, who cares…? Ugh…"

Rumack sank herself into the sofa, unable to contain her rage. Her bleary eyes glared at Suzuno.

"So… You're a Great Demon General and an Archbishop. Maybe a Great Demon Archbishop? *That's* a pretty powerful title. Are you *really* going to the demon side?"

"Ngh…"

"I always thought you kept a prudent distance from the Devil King. But is this, ah, like they say on Earth, 'getting a side piece'?"

"That phrase is both incorrect and *quite* inappropriate! And *please* be sure you don't use that in front of anyone the next time you're in Japan! Where did you even learn that term, General Rumack? I swear…!"

Suzuno had wanted to keep this conversation strictly focused on Maou and Emi. But now she had no choice.

"Let me just say, General Rumack, the only thing I've devoted myself 'heart and soul' to is life in Japan, in general. People might find fault with an Archbishop saying that, but honestly, I find Japan much more agreeable than here."

"Hmph. You mean your setup where you were only separated from the Devil King by a single wall?"

"…I will not deny that. I know this is nothing I should say to a general who fought for her world against the Devil King's Army, but I never had any personal vendetta against that army. If anything, it was the evil present in the human world that made me shrink back. The Devil King may have been an enemy to mankind, but he wasn't an enemy to *me*. And recently, um, I recruited the Devil King to help me organize these feelings in my mind. That was all."

"…That's really all?"

"…It is. I am not lying to you."

"…*Hmmmmmm*…"

Rumack's voice suddenly grew more affable. It made Suzuno feel a chill down her spine.

"I tell you, you need to be a real wordsmith to survive as an Archbishop, don't you?"

"Huh?"

"That's not the subject I was asking about. All I asked was what's *really* behind that incredibly embellished story that you've 'dedicated yourself heart and soul' to the Devil King?"

"I *told* you, there's no truth to that…!"

"Where there's smoke, there's fire, as they say. You said you have no personal grudge against the Devil King. What if you had *more* than that on the opposite side?"

"There are people everywhere trying to start fires where none exist!!"

The exasperated Suzuno and serene Rumack sized each other up a few moments. Rumack looked away first.

"This is silly. I suppose my vision isn't good enough to strip your soul bare. It doesn't look like I'll glean any more from you today."

"Will you *stop* that already?!"

"Because I was *hoping* for something like you stealing Chiho's love while nobody was looking over in Japan."

"…Just stop it!"

"But all right. I understand now."

"General Rumack!"

Rumack suddenly came to her feet and headed for the door, the meeting apparently over in her mind.

"I doubt I'm going to hear anything else that'll assuage Emeralda. If anything, it's just going to make her madder. I probably won't see you again before the day of the summit. In the meantime…"

She eyed Suzuno carefully as she opened the door.

"…Please don't cause any more trouble. My hands are already full enough fending off all the factions who want to visit Japan. They're all trying their damnedest to visit that 'MgRonald' site, recruiting Emilia or the Devil King to their side before the summit begins. It's driving me crazy."

"…"

"If they knew those two, they'd learn that *not* visiting them leaves the best impression of all."

"…But neither of them are going to side with anyone. Not besides Chiho."

"I wonder. *You'll* side with them in the end, too, won't you?"

"Huh?"

"I can't tell you how jealous I am, y'know. Have fun stoking Emeralda's rage."

Whether that was sarcastic or not, it was what Rumack chose to part with as she shut the door behind her.

"…What was *that* all about?"

Rumack had come in and out like a passing storm, cruelly toying with Suzuno. She sat there blankly for a moment, incapable of anything else. One thing, however, she was positive about.

"…It had to be Amane."

Chiho would have been a little more prudent with Emeralda before dropping the news…and Suzuno couldn't think of anyone else in a position to do it.

"I know it was for Acieth's sake, but relying on the Shiba family might be too costly to be worth it… But to think that Emeralda was that angered by it…?"

Now that she was calmer, Suzuno noticed a thing or two Rumack had said that needed addressing.

"As dry as their relationship may seem right now, all it takes is a single unexpected spark to set it aflame…" Rumack had said.

She knew her own heart had followed a similar path. It formed a doubt in her mind that ballooned by the moment, agitating her anew.

"I…I hardly had any dramatic inspiration that made me act, come to think of it… That trigger could come from anywhere, really, whenever it comes up… No, but not *Emilia*, of all people… But…no, I am hardly trying to claim exclusive rights here…"

With Rumack gone, Suzuno writhed on the sofa, no longer caring about how much it'd wrinkle her robe. Now it was clear as day: the hangdog look on Maou's face, the one she saw at the end of everything, built up over time. Some spark in her made her want to support that man…and after that, she couldn't hold her feelings back. In another few moments, she had made her confession.

As she considered her previous actions, she could tell there was no logical argument for any of them. But she knew it'd happened. So who could say that *wouldn't* happen to Emi?

But…it *was* Emi. Suzuno had no personal grudge or negative emotions toward Maou, but Emilia was different. Things might have relaxed a bit after Nord was found alive and well, but for that enmity to disappear, there was just so much Maou had to atone for. There was no possible way things would work out the way Rumack or Emeralda feared. As someone who had watched both of them up close, Suzuno knew that better than anyone.

"So why…?"

Why, indeed? None of this had happened with Chiho. If Chiho

were her rival, Suzuno would've kept as composed as a clear mountain lake. She was proud of that serenity, the result of her diligent clerical study.

"So why did this...?"

But the moment she replaced Chiho with Emi in her mind, where did all these dark emotions come from? They made her heart race, her throat dry up, her limbs hang limply off her body.

"Ugh..."

Her reason, her logic, her knowledge, her memories, her thoughts, her experiences, her environment, her pride as a cleric—all of it told her that she was acting strangely. She was making the wrong moves. But even with all of that together, there was a flame that burned it all up in an instant, setting her impulses and emotions on fire—the flame of jealousy.

"I am such a fool..."

But all the groaning and self-loathing in the world couldn't quell the dark flames Suzuno was experiencing for the first time. She didn't know that in her heart, the one she had analyzed and explained to Chiho, was no all-encompassing platonic love. That inscrutable shape inside her, the one driving her straight down a road lit by flame, was a love driven by deep, dark, all-consuming passion.

✳

"Hmm... So, um, what's important about that?" Urushihara asked.

"What's important? You don't think anything about it?" Laila countered in a huff.

"I *think* you're an asshole for waking me up for no reason, dudette."

"No reason...? Amane came to tell me about it. You don't think that's bad?"

"Oh, yeah, geez, that sucks, huh? Anyway, I'm going to sleep."

"Lucifer, wait!"

Urushihara's nest was located in the midsection of Devil's Castle on the Central Continent. It was once a plain corridor, but he had remodeled it into his personal hideout. From his window he had a commanding view of the outside, but if you looked straight down from it, you could see some kind of giant reptile sleeping there.

"...Look, I get it. From your standpoint, you just got reunited with your daughter, and all of a sudden she's shacked up with this dude. But to *me*, it's like, what's the big surprise at *this* point? If you don't mind my saying so, they've had a date, they've had a sleepover... If people wanna assume whatever kinda sleazy stuff they want, they got all the ammo they need for it. And that's *with* Alas Ramus!"

Laila, since journeying to Devil's Castle with Urushihara to deliver Kinanna, had devoted herself to dealing with the lizard, and working with Lucifer and Gabriel (who were left to tend to the castle) as well as the knights and clerics from the Eastern and Western Islands. In his doddering old age, Kinanna could go for days without moving an inch, only to fly into a hellish rage—it was like a light switch—but he had done nothing but snore for the past two days or so. It was then that Laila received word from Amane about Emi and Maou living together, so she quickly went to inform Urushihara—and *this* was the treatment she'd gotten.

"Besides, this is all probably because some kinda issue with the Yesod is forcing 'em to team up to handle it, right? *We* can't do anything about it, so let's just wait till it blows over and then *they* can tell us all about it! You know Amane gets off on gossiping like that! Why's an angel like you givin' her what she wants, huh?"

"...You know all of that?"

"Chiho Sasaki's up to a lot over here, yeah? Whenever she's up to something, the Yesod fragments always get involved, so I figured somethin' was probably up with Acieth and Alas Ramus. And lemme tell you, if you start jabbing at Emilia about that, you're *really* gonna piss her off, dudette."

"I—I know that, but... Listen, would it be bad if I went back to Japan one time? I, you know, I want to ask my husband why he agreed to it, you could say..."

Urushihara twisted his face even more as he glared at Laila, her motherly concern getting the better of her.

"...Listen. The only people who can directly *do* anything about Kinanna are me, you, Albert, and Gabriel. We got our hands full trying to control the guy without killin' him. If even one of us drops out, you *know* what that's gonna cause, don't you?"

"But I can make up for it..."

"Okay, then find someone else to make up your shifts. I'm not lettin' you take time off."

"I never expected *you* to say something like that! And I'll remind you, by law it's the responsibility of the manager to find shift replacements, not the employee!"

"This is Ente Isla. *I'm* the law right now. And even in Japan, where the hell are you gonna find a boss who actually *does* that?"

Urushihara's voice, despite the discernible fatigue, made it clear Laila was playing with fire. If she decided to skip town, there was no telling how he'd bite back.

"Besides, what's the point of knowing all the details? Don't tell me you're gonna be casing their place, looking for any sign Maou and Emilia are up to stuff?"

"Huh? No! But as her mother, I have a duty to—"

"Where do you get off busting out the 'mother' card after abandoning her for a dozen years or whatever?"

"There... There was a reason for that... That's a different issue..."

"If you're gonna start suspecting her and Maou *that* way, she'll kill you. Seriously, dude, if *I* can see that, why can't *you*? ...Great, and now I'm fully awake. Thanks a lot."

Looking annoyed, Urushihara sat up from the sleeping bag—laid out on the bare stone floor—and yawned, still mostly zipped inside. "You gotta get a clue, Laila," he said as he wiped his eyes, head tilted down. "In theory, at least, Devil's Castle is ready to launch—whether we get the stone in Kinanna's throat or not."

"I—I know that, but—"

"And Chiho Sasaki's getting all worked up about this summit, but do you really think some international meetup organized by a teenage girl is gonna usher in peace in one day? Just think about it! There's no way it's gonna work!"

"Well…yeah…"

"And we haven't even figured out what to do with that heavenly astronaut. You *know* she's not gonna stop with giving the Archbishops those dreams and sending the Church knights for us. If some other force goes crazy and attacks us right this minute, we might have to launch this thing just to evacuate to the demon realms. And *you* wanna go home 'cause you're worried about what kinda guy your daughter's living with? Quit being stupid. If you wanna atone for plunging the world into chaos, think about what needs to come first here."

Urushihara's perfectly valid argument stunned Laila into silence.

"Besides," he added, "we got the Federated Order knights from the South to think about. Maybe they're loyal to Rajid, but they're not like the forces who joined our war from the start. Depending how the summit turns out, we may have to kill 'em all first. If you wanna think about something, think about *that*."

"I… I'm sorry…"

Laila, faced with this impenetrable wall of logic, calmed down, shoulders drooped in shame over her behavior.

"B-but what's gotten into you anyway? Because no offense, but ever since we brought Kinanna here, it's like you've had a total personality change. At first, you'd skip work all the time because you didn't like Alciel lecturing you about repairing Devil's Castle."

"Hey, people grow."

"That's a *really* annoying way to put it…"

Urushihara pretended not to hear that.

"You know, as I've worked here, I've come to have some regrets."

"…Okay, like what?"

"Not to sound all responsible now, but… You know, I still don't really care what happens to this world. But I don't wanna go out of my way to make Alas Ramus cry, and if I wanna have fun right now, I figure, hey, listening to other people for a little while ain't that bad a thing. And I think I'm doing some good work, dude."

"…Well, everything's been put in place a lot faster than planned, I heard…"

"Yeah, 'cause I remembered some stuff."

"I'm wondering what kind of 'stuff' this is."

"Look, dudette, I secured our transport, I got some vital data into my mind, and now I'm riskin' my life dealing with that demented lizard down there. You know about those magic light beams of his. He ain't foolin' around."

"Y-yes, I know, but—"

"And *you're* all like 'ooh, no, Maou and Emilia, wah, wah, wah.' Come on, lady, who cares? We don't really know who that space-suit dude is, and Maou and Emilia are *really* gonna be our main firepower here? We keep having this crap push us back, you know? It's like what Farfarello said once—all humans really care about is themselves…"

His eyes seemed to cloud up as he orated from his sleeping bag.

"So I got some regrets, y'know? I do. Like, I had no idea it'd be so enraging when you're working hard and everyone else is going on about the most useless bullshit. It just makes me wanna lay low and keep quiet. Like moss in the forest, you see?"

"Um… Yes…?"

"Ashiya, y'know, he's a good guy. He tries. But look at you! Do you seriously think Maou and Emilia are gonna *do* anything, living together? They're not! Chiho Sasaki's probably gonna yap about it unless we tell her in advance, but otherwise, there's zip between them! And I'm *never* gonna let you go back to Japan for that, okay?!"

"Okay, okay! I understand! You don't have to shout at me!"

"Ugh! I'm gonna force myself to sleep a little longer, all right? And don't wake me up for stupid crap next time! I don't care about the summit, and if you start telling me about whatever tasty meal Bell and Chiho Sasaki are having, I really *am* gonna get pissed off at you!"

Fully zipped back up and looking a bit like a bagworm, Urushihara wriggled around, rolling on the floor as he groused. His final outburst sent him rolling toward the wall. He opted not to move once he hit it; Laila didn't know if he was hurt or just pouting as he tried to sleep again, but either way, she had now put the idea of returning to Japan well behind her. Instead, all she could do was shrug at the curled-up back of the pouty fallen angel over by the wall.

"But…you know, once this is all over, I'm pretty sure it'll all go back to normal."

*

It was a busy day for everyone hard at work in Ente Isla, and now it was coming to a close.

Maou, for what was likely the first time since he landed on Earth, was using a private bath. While there had been one in the Choshi villa that they'd stayed in during their stint as Ohguro-ya staff, that was really more of an employee dorm.

"Y'know, if you think about it, it's amazing, isn't it? Like, having your own private bathtub in your home."

It wasn't hard to imagine just how revolutionary a concept it was for Maou to not have to visit the traditional local bathhouse to get washed up. This *was* a pretty fancy apartment building, yes, but there was nothing that special about Emi's bathroom. Still, it offered almost too much size and functionality for a solo apartment dweller; even the shape of the faucet was miles ahead of what Maou knew in the public bath. He had listened as Emi explained how everything worked, accepting the towel she'd apparently bought for him in advance.

"That was nice of her," he muttered as he prepared to take a bath, "although I'd guess she just doesn't want me messing up the place… Better not use up too much hot water, either… Man, it's nice being able to shower where you live… The water here feels softer, somehow. It's neat."

The showers at the public bath could surprise you with the force with which they ejected water against your skin, jets going in all sorts of haywire directions due to clogged showerheads. But Emi's shower was more refined, the water from it feeling soft despite the decent amount of water pressure.

"Now, um, she said I could use the shampoo on this shelf?"

He had intended to buy some new toiletries, but once she'd found out that Maou was staying over, Alas Ramus had stayed latched onto him until Emi had finally gotten her to bed at nine in the evening. There was a pharmacy down the street, but it closed at nine, and apparently the local convenience store didn't have much in men's bath amenities. So Emi reluctantly let him use some of the shampoo and body wash on hand, but:

"...Which ones were they again?"

On the shelf were three transparent, unlabeled bottles of soap, all looking about the same. Presumably she bought some bottles she liked at the 100-yen shop and purchased soap refills for them, but apart from the different quantities in each one, Maou had no way of telling one from the other.

"Hmm... Oh, is there writing on here? 'Green Echo Bottle'... Oh, it's the brand of the *bottle*?"

It was a fruitless effort. But Emi was busy guiding Alas Ramus to sleep, and he wasn't going to ask her in the buff anyway. Alas Ramus was being pretty obstinate tonight, despite being assured that Daddy would still be around tomorrow. If Maou spoke up right now, there's no telling how Emi would lecture him.

"I think she said 'shampoo, conditioner, and body soap from the right'... Hmm? Or was it from the left? ...Well, whatever."

Making a guess at it, Maou got under the shower and gave the right-hand bottle a shot. The color and aroma of the gel-like liquid was nothing he had seen before, and it certainly wasn't giving him any clues. So he ran it through his hair.

"...Ah."

It wasn't foaming. So the bottle on the right was conditioner. He could already hear Emi jabbing at him.

"Damn it..."

The only hair-care products he knew were the cheap shampoo he bought and whatever came out of the spigot in the public bath. He had never used standalone conditioner before. The presence of *three* or so bottles was unexpected in itself.

"...Well, hmm."

But by process of elimination, either of the two bottles had to give him foam.

"Normally, you'd put the two hair-care products next to each other, right…?"

So from the left, it was probably body soap, shampoo, then conditioner. His first guess was completely wrong.

"But I'm not brave enough to ask now, and it's gotta be nicer than the stuff I use anyway. Let's just go with this…and I'll buy my own tomorrow."

Thus, figuring it best to avoid attracting Emi's ire, he washed his hair and body with whatever happened to bubble up for him. He felt fresher, if fairly guilty, as he left the bath and put on some underwear, shorts, and a T-shirt for bed purposes. Then he took a look around.

"Oooh…"

There was a bar of soap and a cup for toothbrushes at the washbasin, but no hair dryer was in sight. She probably put it in one cabinet or another, but he didn't want to rifle through everything and get yelled at.

"…Hey, Emi?"

Instead, he decided it'd be quicker and safer to just ask. He kept it to a loud whisper, trying to avoid waking up Alas Ramus.

"…What is it?" came the response, sounding surprisingly close. She must've put the child to bed. The sound from the TV was still faintly audible.

"Do you have a hair dryer?"

"Oh, I didn't mention that… You decent?"

"Yeah."

"…"

She entered the bathroom, taking out a surprisingly large handheld hair dryer from the cabinet next to the mirror. "The outlet's over there," she said as she turned to leave.

"…"

Then she turned back, opening the door again and looking into the bathroom.

"What? Did I do something wrong?"

Given how snippy Emi had been lately (a real throwback to the past), Maou was on pins and needles around her.

"Yeah, I guess I really need to check up on these things, huh?"

"What?"

"...You normally use a bathhouse all the time, right?"

"Y-yeah."

"Well, with a home bath, a lot of hair flies around, you know."

"Hair?"

Emi pointed at the floor around the shower. Short clippings of hair were all over the wet tile.

"You don't need to do a full cleaning, but try to wash all that off before you go."

"A-all right. Sorry."

"It's all right. You didn't know. And make sure to turn the ventilation fan on before you leave—the mold sets in fast otherwise. Also..."

"There's more?"

"You see the roller over there? If you could use that to pick up whatever hair's lying around after you're done drying, that'd be great."

After tacking on those extra rules, Emi left Maou alone, holding her expensive-looking hair dryer.

"...This is gonna be harder than I thought," he mourned as he got to work, the fancy dryer actually far weaker and colder than the one at the public bath. After that, he used the roller to pick up whatever hair he noticed around him.

"Ahh..."

Now came the question of what to do with the wet towel and dirty laundry. Just as the thought occurred to him, Emi knocked on the door and came in.

"Sorry, but can you put your dirty laundry in here for today?" she asked, brandishing a large grocery-store plastic bag. "There's a basket by the washer, but we'll get your own tomorrow."

"We're gonna do separate loads?"

"Of course. I use different detergents for Alas Ramus and myself, but if you've got your own preference, make sure to buy that. If not, you can use mine."

"Oh, no, I don't care. Like, normally I just use soap powder. But…"

"What?"

"Are you sure I can use all this stuff of yours?"

The question, simply reflexive, was greeted with a glare.

"The important thing right now is the 'family' atmosphere we're supposed to be making with Alas Ramus, isn't it?"

"Oh… Yeah."

"If I made you keep *everything* separate from me, that'd be weird, don't you think? And if I was gonna take it to extremes, I'd ask you to use a separate washer anyway, so…"

"Yeah, I bet," replied Maou as he obediently put his clothes in the bag.

"I get that you're nervous, but let's both just try to deal with it, okay? I'll try not to be colder with you than I have to be. And I know it won't be for *that* long, but Alas Ramus is here, so let's try not to get in any arguments we don't have to. Let me know if you have any other questions."

With that, Emi let him alone once more.

"…Y'know, when push comes to shove, she's a lot more mature than I am."

Given how dead set against it she was at first, it almost seemed anticlimactic to Maou.

Then bedtime rolled around.

"It's kind of weird, isn't it?" he asked.

"What do you want from me? After thinking it over, this was the best solution I came up with. It's what I had Eme do when she was here."

At half-past ten, the bedding was all laid out. Maou had assumed he'd just wrap himself in a blanket and sleep on the floor or something while Emi and Alas Ramus used their bed, but when he got out of the bath, he found Alas Ramus sprawled out in the bed and a pair of futons rolled out next to each other on the floor nearby.

"You can use the one farthest from the bed. If Alas Ramus asks for something in the middle of the night, you wouldn't know what to do, would you?"

"N-no... Yeah."

It threw Maou for a loop. He never expected in a million years that Emi would provide a futon for him.

"You can hop in first. I'll go take a bath."

"Okay..."

Emi left Maou sitting on his futon as she went to the bathroom. After about half an hour in there, she turned out the living-room light and joined him in the bedroom. She had changed into a loose lemon-yellow T-shirt and shorts, which were apparently her night clothes.

"You still awake?"

"Yeah, um... Sorry, I need to charge my phone."

"...Oh." Emi nodded, then pointed toward the window. "It's kind of far away, but that's the only outlet."

"Ah... Thanks."

Maou crouched down windowside and plugged his phone in.

"Well, good night," Emi said, going into the middle futon. Maou did the same with his, still feeling a bit agitated, trying to be silent and turning his back to the women. The futon and sheets felt freshly washed, the comforter lighter than anything he had experienced but still nice and warm. After he'd spent the day playing with Alas Ramus and gotten exposed to all these unfamiliar things, fatigue quickly overcame him—but there was one more thing he had to say. Summoning his resolve, he spoke up, back still turned.

"Hey, Emi?"

"...What?" she replied, not turning around.

"Um...I'm sorry."

"About what?"

There was a slight element of surprise in the reaction to his sudden apology.

"...You know, when you stayed at my place...like, way before any of this happened..."

"You mean when we were fighting off Gabriel?"

"Yeah... That. We made you sleep right on the tatami floor, didn't we?"

"Oh, yeah, you did. I forgot until you mentioned it. What about it?"

"Well, um, you've done so much for me today, now I feel kinda sorry about it, so...I just wanted to say that."

"..."

Emi seemed confused for a moment. Then he felt her turn over. From the sound of her heavy sigh, she was on her back now.

"That's what you have to say to me? Things are a lot different now from then, aren't they."

"Yeah, they are, but still..."

"And both times, we did that because we had to, right? There's no problem to speak of, so it's fine. Okay? We gotta get up early tomorrow."

"Y-yeah, right. Sorry."

"Mm. Oh, also..."

"Hmm?"

"I told you Amane would contact them...but I'll talk things over with Chiho and Bell, too, okay?"

"...Sure."

"Or would you prefer I didn't?"

"Well, we can't really avoid it..."

"I know it might be hard for you, so I'll look for an opportunity to... Again, good night."

"...Yeah."

A little while later, Emi began to lightly snore, joining Alas Ramus next to her. Maou could occasionally hear an emergency vehicle's siren out the window. Sensing all that, he reflected back on the past day...

"...sssp..."

...and in short time, he quietly joined them.

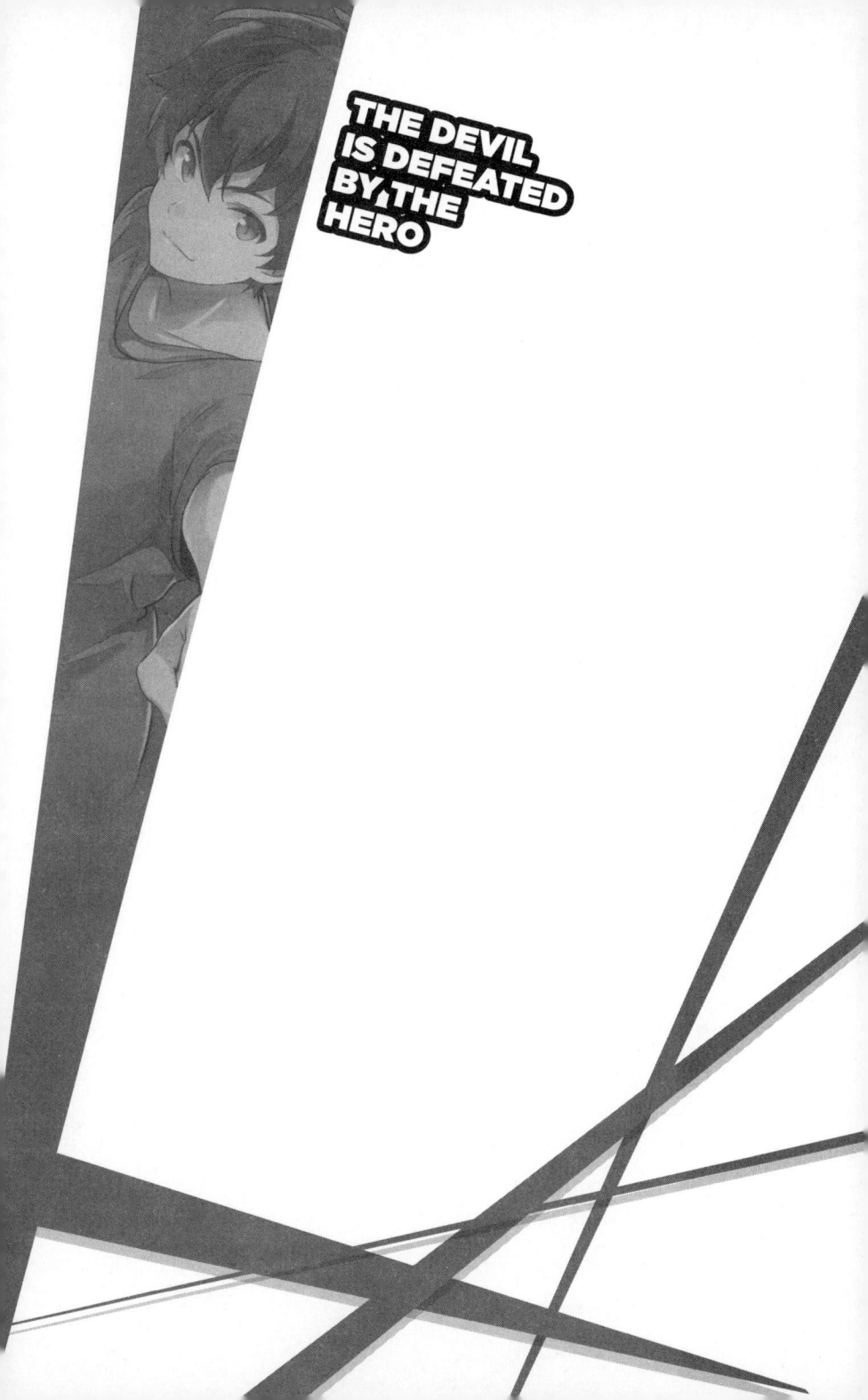

"Here you go…"

Preparing the best tea she had around the house, Riho gingerly offered a cup to her guest—a woman smaller than her, but nonetheless about the same age. Someone she knew well.

"Oh, thank youuu! I'm so sorry to drop in this late at niiight…"

"No, it's…fine."

"Not to pryyy, but is your husband here?"

Riho understood what her guest was driving at. "No, he won't be around for a while."

"…All riiight," came the reply with a nod. "Again, sorry to bother you. I'll leave as soon as my duty is done here. If I'm in the way, I could wait in your daughter's bedroom instead…?"

The offer was sincere. Riho mulled for a moment, then sat across from her guest and shook her head. "…No, you can wait here. It's pretty normal for a father not to know her daughter's friends…and she might get angry if I let someone into her room without permission."

"…All right. Thank you."

The guest, understanding Riho's logic, bowed her head a bit. It was a little past ten in the evening, much too late for an informal gathering like this.

A new voice came in through the entrance. "Hi! Boy, am I tired... Hey, Mom, I'm hungry—huh?"

"Hellooo."

"Emeralda? What's up?"

Chiho, fresh from her prep school, was ready to relax after a long day, only to be surprised by Emeralda's presence. The sorcerer, dressed in her palace robes, gave Chiho a grand bow, the sort one delivered to a member of Saint Aile nobility—something far more formal than what she gave Riho.

"Madam Chairman," she said, head still down, "please forgive me for calling so late at night, and without warning."

"E-Emeralda?!"

"I know, as a member of a summit, such behavior deserves to be criticized...but I received the permission of Ms. Shiba to make the trip, and of your mother to wait for you here."

"Um, okay..."

Chiho stood there confused for a moment, bag still on her shoulder.

"Ms. Shiba...? The landlord, you mean, or Amane?"

"Ms. Shiba put in a good word for me through Amane Ohguro."

"Ch-Chiho...?" Riho wasn't sure what to make of the atmosphere between Emeralda and Chiho. She froze, half-standing up from her seat.

"..."

But the intensity melted from Chiho's face the moment she heard Emeralda's reply.

"Oh, Amane... Why *now*, after everything...?"

She shrugged, now looking several times more exhausted than before. Then she turned her back to the still-bowed Emeralda.

"Would you like to talk in my room? Or...would you like to go look now?" Chiho asked.

Emeralda grinned. "Not to ask in front of your motherrr, but would you like to go enjoy the niiightlife a little?"

"Uhh...Mom?"

"Y-yes?"

"We're gonna go out on a walk, so could you lock the window in my room after we go?"

"Huh? The window?"

One minute later, Riho watched out her own bedroom window as her daughter disappeared into the night sky on Emeralda's back. Chiho was concerned, apparently, that going out at night with Emeralda dressed as she was would attract undue attention from the authorities.

"…This isn't what I would call 'enjoying the nightlife,' exactly…"

As a mother, she couldn't erase her concern.

"I hope she'll at least come *back* through the front door."

✳

"I'm truuuly sorry! When I heard about it, I just couldn't stay puuut!"

Emeralda's voice didn't make her sound very sorry as it floated across the night air. Chiho rolled her eyes and gave her a pinch on the cheek.

"Aren't *you* the one who told all the members not to contact me more than strictly necessary? If everyone else finds out, don't expect me to defend you."

"That's fiiine. I'm speciaaal! You may not remember, since you've known Emilia and the Devil King for a whiiile, but if push comes to shove, I'm at least as powerful as Emiliaaa! Like a tactical nuuuke!"

"…And the scary part is that it's true, huh? I know what you mean, but right now…"

"Yes, yes, I knooow. I know, but…" Emeralda's expression froze, making the night air seem all the more frigid. "*Thiiiis* time… I simply can-*noooooot* accept this… Really, I'm surprised you can keep your temmmper right now, Chiho."

"Ugh… Amane's *way* out of line…"

Emeralda Etuva was one of the keystones of the "Second Invasion" of Devil's Castle planned out by Chiho, as well as a member of the summit. She may not have as powerful a political post as the other participants, but her history as a companion to the Hero more than made up for that. They may not stand out as much in their political roles, but Emeralda and Albert, while not as powerful as Emi, were very much a tactical-level force in Ente Isla. And if someone at that level was reaching out to the chairman of the summit meant to work out what postwar Ente Isla would look like, there had to be one reason for that.

"Do Suzuno and Ashiya know about this?"

"Hmmm? That I'm here in Japaaan? Orrr..."

Emeralda turned her head around, smiling like a crazed snake.

"...that Emilia, a woman I value more than my liiife, has been living with the Devil King for *quite* a long tiiime now?"

"Did Amane phrase it like *that*? Uggghhh...!"

Amane had to be the leak. Chiho knew that upon realizing Amane was playing customs agent between the two worlds...and if Suzuno knew, that probably meant that Amane had told everyone she could get in contact with. Emeralda had her doubts about it precisely because she knew how Chiho, Maou, and Emi's relationship worked—but to Chiho, the idea of Maou and Emi living together was actually welcome, if it got them all that much closer to her own aims. That's why Chiho hadn't panicked when Suzuno contacted her about it from Ente Isla—in fact, it helped her settle on her strategy for the upcoming summit.

"...It's still before eleven. I think Maou and Yusa are closing tonight, but where are you going to wait for them?"

"Where eeelse? I know the *perfect* spot over there, don't I?"

"Agh!"

With that, Emeralda made a nosedive for the neighborhood of Hatagaya.

They landed in a deserted alley behind a mixed-use building, then walked right through the door of a certain nearby establishment.

"Good evening— Hmm?"

The man behind the counter welcomed them with a quizzical look.

"Chiho Sasaki? Why are you here so late? ...Ah."

Mitsuki Sarue, manager at Sentucky Fried Chicken, lifted his eyebrows at the sight of Chiho and her partner.

"...Are you Emeralda Etuva, then?" he asked, surprised all over again.

"Hellooo, Archangel Sarielll! I hope you're doing well. I had a little bizzzness in the area, so we'll just sit here until clooosing time, okay? Oh, Chiho, can you order me some maple cookies and hot tea with miiilk? You can get what you want with thiiis."

Emeralda took out a ten-thousand-yen bill—where she got it from, nobody knew—and handed it to Chiho before walking toward a booth. Chiho watched her go, then turned toward Sariel...only to be startled by his reproachful look.

"Chiho Sasaki... I know a pretty strange crowd's been shuffling through MgRonald lately. What did you do *this* time?"

"Oh, ah, uh... Nothing?"

"Do you think you're convincing me at all? Or would you like me to have you read my full report on how it felt to have Ms. Kisaki call me by my real name over the phone?"

"I—I'm sorry..."

"Look, whatever you're up to, I'm not gonna interfere. I'm not going to get involved at all, in fact! *But!* If you mess with the happy future Ms. Kisaki and I will have, you'll pay dearly for it!"

"Ah, I'm sorry, I'm sorry! I'll be more careful, okay?!"

As much as she wanted to question how probable that "happy future" was, Chiho knew now wasn't the time. This was her fault, after all.

"Careful or not, I can't have this happen again, all right? So! One order of maple cookies, one hot tea with milk, and what do you want—*mmph!*"

"Hyah?!"

Suddenly, Sariel was slapped in the back of the head with something brown and plastic. It was an SFC tray, and a female employee was wielding it behind him.

"Why are you being so rude to a customer?"

"F…Furuya…"

The woman he called Furuya pushed his wide-eyed face to the side and stood in front of Chiho.

"Please excuse Mr. Sarue, my manager. May I take your order?"

"Oh, ah, um, I—I'll just have an Original Chicken set…"

Her name tag read KANAKO FURUYA, a name Chiho was familiar with—she had heard that Furuya was the only SFC team member who knew how to keep Sariel under control. The moment she saw the name, she wound up going for a full value meal, the concept of occupying a booth all night with nothing but a small drink making her feel too guilty.

"Okay, we'll have that out for you right away… *Move* it, Manager!"

"Nnngh…"

Sariel groaned as he began preparing the order. Chiho wondered who the manager *really* was around here, but as she did, Furuya spoke up again.

"……You're Chiho Sasaki, right?"

"Huh?"

"I think this is the first time we've had a chance to speak. My name's Furuya, and I'm a shift manager at the Hatagaya SFC."

"Ah…"

"I heard that you and Mr. Maou took care of Sarue during his visits to MgRonald since back when Ms. Kisaki was running things. Let me apologize for all the trouble he's caused."

"N-no, um, he's a customer like anyone else, and, uh, he's really not a bad person or anything, so…"

"Maybe not, but he's a *mystery* man, you know? He has a lot of secrets. And at the same time, he's always letting his guard down."

It sounded so natural, flowing out from Kanako, that Chiho almost missed it entirely—but the meaning behind the words said a lot to her.

"M…Ms. Furuya…? What do you mean by that…?"

"Well, Akiko Ohki and I actually go back a number of years. That, and I know Ms. Kisaki called Sarue a few days ago about some sort of…news that unnerved him. I wheedled the truth out of him, and he just said she was confirming something she didn't have a chance to ask him before now. The way he acted, you'd think she caught him cheating on his wife or something. He was worthless the rest of the shift that day. It was just exasperating!"

"Oh…um…"

Chiho froze. This wasn't what she'd expected. Kanako knew Akiko well; Sariel was freaking out a few days ago; he said something about it to Kanako; and now she was speaking in riddles to Chiho, a girl she wouldn't have known much. Chiho wasn't dumb enough to think all these coincidences in a row didn't mean anything.

"Ms. Sasaki?"

"Y-yes?!"

"Your order's ready right here."

Realizing her chicken value meal was waiting for her, Chiho hurriedly picked it up.

"Enjoy…"

Somehow maintaining his composure as an SFC employee, Sariel retired back to the kitchen. Chiho saw him go, then—quickly snapping out of it—took her tray with a light bow and stepped away from the counter.

"Um, sorry to bother you during work…"

"Not at all. Oh, and Ms. Sasaki?"

"Yes?!"

But she was stopped once again.

"To tell the truth, you know, I've been doing this part-time since I was in high school."

"Uh-huh…"

"I first took this job at a location in Hatsudai, close to Shinjuku, but then they opened this spot near my home and I joined the opening crew."

Hatsudai was a station on the Keio New Line, a private rail link connecting to the Toei Shinjuku line. It was just one stop away from Hatagaya.

"Oh, you did?"

Chiho wasn't sure where was this going. Then Kanako gave her a wink.

"So about a month after I took the job at Hatsudai, the MgRonald here in Hatagaya started taking applications. The SFC in Hatsudai was close to my high school, but I live in Hatagaya, so I remember feeling like 'Oh man, I messed up.'"

"Oh?"

"Like, 'If I had chosen MgRonald, where would I be right now?' kind of thing. Hee-hee…"

Chiho smiled faintly, but kept her guard up. She was no longer the kind of irresolute, weak-hearted girl to let this throw her.

"Ms. Furuya?"

"Yes?"

"Can you tell Mr. Sarue to stop letting private issues outside of work faze him?"

Kanako looked kind of embarrassed for a moment, but quickly grinned and gave her a bow.

"Enjoy your meal!"

Chiho quickly headed back to the booth her companion sat at. Kanako watched her go, looking at the odd clothing on her partner.

"I still find it hard to believe, in a lot of ways…but it'd be neat if it's true. But meanwhile…"

She turned back toward the kitchen, where the weary-looking Mitsuki Sarue toiled inside.

"…Ugh."

Kanako sighed a bit, then smiled to herself.

"Meanwhile, I get stuck with *this* guy. It just doesn't make sense."

"Did you discusssss something?"

"Oh, um, that employee's name is Furuya. She knows a lot of the MgRonald staff thanks to all of Sariel's nonsense, so I told her about me quitting and stuff."

"Ohhh, I see."

With her sharp ears and the mostly empty dining space at SPC, Emeralda should've been able to listen in on Chiho and Furuya's conversation. But Kanako Furuya wasn't going to have any huge impact on Chiho's and Emeralda's futures, and even if she did overhear them, Emeralda had bigger fish to fry at the moment.

"Sooo..."

"Yes?"

"I've been hearing a lot about what's up with the Sephiraaah, and the Yesssod, and so forth. But even after asking Bell, and Amaaane, there's still something I'm not very cleeear on."

"Um, just to be sure, is it about Yusa and Maou living together?"

"Huh?"

The sudden question threw Emeralda for a loop. She'd already stated this was the topic for the evening, and now Chiho was confirming it again.

"Well, yesss, but..."

"All right. So, what about it?"

"*Youuu're* okay with it...?!"

"Okay with Yusa and Maou living together?"

"Isn't that what I just saaaid?"

Chiho seemed hell-bent on making this conversation go nowhere. It put Emeralda into a rare state of irritation.

"You know what I meeean, right, Chiho? You're not a chiiild."

"...I'm sorry, I'm not sure I do."

"Well, you know, Chiho..." The air around them chilled. "I could understand the Devil King being near to Emilia. But would I tolerate it? No. Not for a single second."

"..."

"And if you want to spend your days with the Devil King, then by all means, do whatever you like. If the Devil King is willing to live out his days here in Japan, then fine by me. But..."

Emeralda had now flung off her usual softened demeanor. She glared at Chiho.

"But if you're not willing to serve as the chains that bind the Devil King to this world, then I'm afraid it's over."

After a long pause, Chiho said, "......Emeralda?"

"Yes?"

"...First, let me apologize to you. I had Lady Wurs give me profiles on all the summit attendees."

"...Hee-hee." That was all the information Emeralda needed for something to dawn in her mind. "Ahh, there's no beating that old biddy, is there?"

It wasn't at all like Emeralda. Her face was full of anger as she bit her lip. Chiho gracefully accepted it.

"Emeralda... I understand...you lost your family to the Devil King's Army as well?"

Before then, Chiho knew nothing at all about Emeralda's past. She knew it wasn't the kind of thing Emeralda was eager to discuss. But until things came to this, knowing nothing about the scars borne by a good friend from another world always seemed like a mistake to Chiho.

Emeralda, for her part, wasn't simple-minded enough to let this cloud her mind.

"It's not that rare of a thing. I don't know if you heard, but the same is true for Olba, and for Cervantes as well. Al, even."

"..."

"But did you hear about this? When Lucifer's forces rolled into the imperial capital, I...I decided to fully abandon my father's territories."

"...Yes, I did."

"Good. That saves me some time."

Emeralda took a deep breath, repositioning herself in her seat.

"I was the eldest child of the lord of a decently sized parcel of rural land in Saint Aile. It was out in the country, but our land made a lot of money, so our family always had this 'nouveau riche' approach to life. But given the background we had, we knew all too well how important a good education was. Where I come from, it's a given that the male heirs inherit the family fortunes. But they still sent me to a university in the capital, and I'll tell you, they had no reason to other than their love for me. *That's* the kind of family I decided to abandon."

"..."

"This was after the decision came that it was impossible to fully defend against the Lucifer force's offensive. But the Church knights were still as revved-up as ever. During the fighting in the imperial capital, I deliberately shot a bolt of magic at our cathedral. I was frustrated—is *this* the best our so-called disciples of God can do? But we had word that Adramelech's forces were approaching from the north. The dominant thought in my mind was, you know, if we send reinforcements to our frontier settlements, we could lose the capital…and in the end, I wound up taken prisoner by Lucifer's forces."

Emeralda took a big bite out of a maple cookie with her dainty lips.

"It took a while for me to understand what I had done. It didn't fully hit me until after Lucifer was defeated and I began traveling with Emilia… The first time I visited Sloane."

"Sloane… Where Yusa came from?"

"Emilia hadn't really fully taken on her mission as the Hero yet. When she saw the burned-out remains of the village, she cried the whole night through. Calling for her father, and the names of all the people she knew… And that made me realize: The people I abandoned, they must have been crying out someone's name as well, as they died there."

"..."

"But as a central government figure, I made the decision to abandon my family and homeland. The decision itself, I don't regret making. I *am* part of nobility. If I played favorites in saving my own kin, it'd be a brutal blow to our family's honor. Maybe you wouldn't understand the nature of how that works, growing up in Japan, but that was the norm over there. But…"

She nibbled on the cookie, tears beginning to form in her eyes.

"But I couldn't abandon my grudge. I couldn't make the hate go away. I don't regret the coolheaded politician side of me, but if your entire family is killed, you're never going to forgive who did it, no matter what the reason was. I had these two polarized sides of me, fighting against each other...and it took protecting Emilia, this sacrifice presented to the Devil King's Army, to make me whole again. This powerless girl, made into a Hero because of her birth. We were all weak, so we placed everything on her instead. Would you believe that, when she defeated Lucifer, Emilia was even smaller than *you* are right now, Chiho?"

"...And that's why you can't allow Yusa to live with Maou?"

"...No." Emeralda shook her head. "I don't really know. Seeing Emilia collapse in tears that day was just crushing to me, but I still don't know what to do. You say it's for Alas Ramus's sake. That's basically for the world's sake, and if you take the long view, maybe it *would* help the world. But...still..." She crushed the cookie in her hand. "Thinking about even the off chance that the hand of Satan, the Devil King, might touch Emilia makes me feel like my heart's going to explode. The politician side of me says to just calm down and watch. That nothing's going to happen."

"Emeralda..."

"But the *real* me...the me that's left in this place free of all obligation... Seeing this man who took my homeland and broke my heart in two, being audacious enough to live under the same roof as the woman I swore to protect with my life... The real me is screaming that she's never going to accept that."

Chiho sat there, taking the quiet, stern words of the most powerful sorcerer in Ente Isla.

"There's no way that Alas Ramus is ever going to cozy up to me. Regardless of how true it really is, that's...the child of Emilia and the Devil King. I just can't find love for that child. I can't shake off the notion that she's the daughter of the Devil King—something that...that Emilia herself has accepted."

Emeralda wasn't openly hostile to Alas Ramus, but the child often reacted quite defensively at her displays of emotion. There were times when she even hid from Emeralda behind Emi. Nobody could know whether Emeralda was right about why, but she must have been very confident about it.

"So what am I supposed to do? You have feelings for the Devil King. Why are you willing to let him spend time with another woman? Why?"

It sounded like Emeralda was condemning her—but then again, maybe she was simply asking a question. Either way, it felt to Chiho like this was the first time Emeralda was speaking to her as a real, breathing human being. But the answer had established itself in Chiho's mind long ago—maybe even before the battle against heaven began.

"You know, Emeralda, the reason I kept asking you whether this was about Maou and Yusa..."

"...Yes?"

"It's because I thought maybe you had an insight into my true feelings."

"You're giving me too much credit. Honestly, I'm not sure I understand what you're thinking at all lately."

"Well, until fairly recently, I really wasn't much more than a leech on Maou and the others."

"...I wouldn't go that far."

Something about Chiho's aura had definitely changed in recent weeks. At the very least, she seemed not at all like the fleeting, unreliable girl Emeralda thought she was at their first meeting. She was bolder now—Emeralda wondered if she had learned that from Wurs—and she had more of a determined, stubborn streak.

"But in a way, I couldn't help that. Lately I'm not sure what Maou and everyone else are thinking, and... Well, everyone's all disconnected about what'll happen after we help Alas Ramus's friends."

"Disconnected?"

"...Yeah." Chiho nodded, picked up the fry container from her meal, and dumped out the contents on her tray. "Like this."

"..."

"I think Ashiya's making a concerted effort to find permanent places around the world for demons to live in. Suzuno… I haven't asked her, but I'm sure she can't just quit being Archbishop that easily. Yusa might decide to go to college in Japan, but she might decide to start up her farm in Ente Isla again. Urushihara… Well, I don't know *what's* on his mind, but I'm sure he'll be happy anywhere he can just laze around and not care about things."

"…And the Devil King?"

"Maou's the worst of all. He's just aimlessly wandering around."

Chiho picked up a fry—maybe seeing it as Maou in her mind—and tossed it into her mouth.

"He talks about getting a full-time job in Japan, but I think he really does want to help with Ms. Kisaki's café. And I think he cares about the demons he rules over, too, although it's really Ashiya running things in that department. He still hasn't given me an answer, and now he's running away from Suzuno's feelings, too. And, you know, once we save Alas Ramus's friends, what's going to happen to Alas Ramus? We don't know. Maybe she'll live with her friends, maybe she'll remain with Yusa…or maybe Maou and Yusa really *will* get married. You know?"

"…I know it's too late, but don't you think you should just give up on that man?"

"That would be like asking you to give up on making Yusa happy, Emeralda. We're all human. We walk the line between rational and irrational behavior."

Chiho gathered up the fries on the tray and ferried them back to the container.

"And *this* is what I want to have happen."

"…Put everything back where it was?"

"No," she said, tapping the box with a finger. "I want some kind of… I don't know, place, or atmosphere, where we can all gather together like this."

"…"

"I could try to hold them down, but apart from Urushihara, they all have different stuff they want to do. That's true now, of course, but there's no reason why *I* have to be the only one accepting them for who they are. I want *them* to accept my feelings, too. That's why I've been striking back at them."

Chiho looked straight at Emeralda.

"And I apologize, Emeralda, but Maou and Yusa living together helps Alas Ramus, it helps Acieth, and it helps me with my future goals. And so I'm not going to stop them."

"...!"

"...And in place of that...I'm ready to accept your feelings, too."

"What do you mean? Are you giving me special consideration at the summit?"

"Oh, no. But I want to do something like thank you, yes. I mean, if you and Albert hadn't made the huge decision to leave Maou alone back then, I'm sure my life would be completely different."

Right after Chiho had learned the truth about Maou, when Emeralda and Albert came to regroup with Emi, they'd agreed to respect her decision to leave Maou alone and not erase Chiho's memories. If they hadn't offered their support, Chiho would almost certainly be just another teenage girl in the crowd right now.

"...It feels like quite a long time ago, doesn't it?"

"I guess time really does go by faster when you grow up, huh?"

"Oh, please, you're not even twenty yet." Emeralda sank into her seat, a little dumbfounded. "...So what are you doing to do for me, exactly?"

"It's nothing big, really. I get regular updates from Amane, you know, so I know about what's going on with Alas Ramus and Acieth and the people around them. So I can talk about that. And I also wanna give you advice along the lines of, like, why not try doing something neither me, nor Suzuno, nor Ashiya, not even Nord have done?"

"...Huh?"

Emeralda raised an eyebrow. In response, Chiho pointed at the MgRonald across the street.

"What I'm saying is, if you're against them living together, you should go right up to them and tell them what you just told me. You're much more deeply connected with Yusa than I am. There's no way she wouldn't seriously consider what you say."

An hour later, close to midnight, the lights dimmed at MgRonald—Chiho and Emeralda's cue to leave.

"...Why do I have to go around with you, huh?" Sariel grumbled.

"It'd be careless *not* to take you," Chiho said.

In a corner of a small path overlooking both MgRonald and Sentucky Fried Chicken, Chiho and Sariel watched Emeralda make her move. After a bit, they saw Maou and Emi exit the restaurant. They looked clearly surprised to find Emeralda there.

"...Wow, they look like a cheating couple after the detective finds them," Chiho said.

"...Pfft. Now Emilia's making excuses for their arrangement." Despite being a hundred yards or so away, Sariel could overhear their conversation. "Devil Kings and Heroes living together... The Apocalypse is upon us."

"Yes. That and an archangel's snooping on people."

"Chiho..."

"Yes?"

"I heard you talking things over with Emeralda, but are you serious?"

"About what?"

"About assembling all the big names of Ente Isla under one big banner?"

"That's my intention."

"Do you think that's even possible? You know what happens when mob rule sets in."

"Yes, I do. I'm college-bound, so I've had to study world history and politics and stuff."

"Hmm?"

"I think people in Ente Isla might have the wrong idea about this…but I feel like everybody's assuming I'm gonna do everything by myself."

"You're not? Because from what I heard, aren't you and Dhin Dhem Wurs planning something together?"

"Well, yes, she's helped set the stage for me…but that just shows I'm not going it alone, right? It's her exercising her own power. Like…"

Chiho shrugged a little.

"It's not like a teenage girl can shout 'Listen to me whine, please' and all these VIPs are going to listen to her. In a war, if you win, you can make a lot of money off it. No leader's going to bow out of it because a girl from some other country—or some other world—tells them to stop. That's why Emeralda said what she did."

"…"

Sariel gave Chiho a look of honest surprise as he continued watching the trio in front of them. "I wasn't going to go that far…but you're that much of a realist about this?"

"This happened more directly because of Suzuno, besides. Or Maou, too, really."

"Hmm?"

"But anyway…I don't want them to give up on living together just because Emeralda yelled at them. In fact, if they do, that's trouble for me."

"Not that I should say this…but with men and women, there's a lot about how they interact that's got nothing to do with logic at all."

"You're right. I never thought Ms. Kisaki would ask you for help, for example."

"…Come on."

"But I understand it."

"Yeah?"

"In terms of emotions, there's no telling. But the thing Emeralda's worried about—something happening between Maou and Yusa—that'll never happen."

"How do you know that?"

"Why wouldn't I?"

Chiho flashed Sariel a smile deeper than any he had seen from her before.

"If that were true, he wouldn't be running away from me and Suzuno now."

"…?"

"Oh!"

Just then, a thoroughly dispirited-looking Emeralda came back.

"No good?"

"…Hmph," she snorted. "It's fiiine. The Devil King was squirming sooo much about it…so I decided to let him beee."

Chiho wasn't sure what Emeralda meant. She looked to Sariel—but either he didn't hear or he didn't want to say, because he offered nothing to her.

"I really resent you, Chihooo…"

"Huh?"

"Talk about getting worked up over nooothing. It sounds like Emiiilia is choosing a man over our friennndship."

"Oh, don't say that, Emeralda," Chiho said with a chuckle as she gave her a hug. "It'll be fine. I know that Yusa is closer to you than to anybody else."

"Ahh… If you say thaaat to me, Chiho, you make it sound like I'm the only unreeeasonable one here…"

Emeralda sobbed a little in her arms.

"But she's a great woman. She's much more honest than I am."

"Ohhh…"

"Hey, can I go?"

Sariel, not bothering to hide his awkwardness, took an Urushihara-style approach to escaping it. But Chiho looked at him as she stroked Emeralda's back, and glumly shook her head no.

"I'm sorry… Can you stay a bit longer?"

"…Is there something else going on?"

"Yes." She nodded, lifting Emeralda's face up. "I want you to see what Yusa probably didn't tell her. The other reason why they have to live together."

* * *

Maou and Emi plodded along the Koshu-Kaido road to Sasazuka Station. Chiho, Emeralda, and Sariel followed behind them, neither Maou nor anyone passing them by taking notice, because Sariel had deployed a dimensional phase barrier, rendering the three of them invisible. It was near midnight, the last train to Eifukucho arriving soon, but neither Maou nor Emi was particularly hurried.

"Well," reasoned Sariel, "if he's got his apartment, I suppose they don't *have* to go back to Emilia's place."

Chiho shook her head. "It's not that. They try to avoid taking things like trains where they'll be seen by other people. Most of the people at MgRonald know, so that's fine, but if something happens to them on a train, there's no talking their way out of that."

"'Talking their way out'? What do you meeean?"

Chiho simply pointed at the pair in front of them.

"It's not necessarily a given, but… Ah."

"Ahh?!"

The moment Chiho turned her attention toward her own hand, Emeralda let out a shout. Emi had suddenly pulled Maou into an alleyway between the buildings lining the street.

"Wh-wh-what are those two doing in there?!"

It was so sudden that Emeralda almost tore right out of the barrier. Chiho's hand stopped her.

"Wait a minute! This is the other reason why they can't call it off!"

On the hand Chiho had used to grab Emeralda's robe was a ring with a stone. That stone was emitting a faint purple glow.

"…Whoa, what's going on with that?"

The next moment, a flash of purple light burst out from the alley the pair ducked into, and then:

"Is…is that…? Chiho, tell me that's not…?"

"…They can't have *that* happening on a train, right? I guess she's defied Yusa's will now and then before, but lately it's been happening a whole bunch. Amane and Yusa both told me about it."

The first figure to emerge from the alley was neither Maou nor Emi. It was a girl about as tall as Emi's shoulders, wearing a long, light-yellow dress. Her hair was as silvery as the Milky Way, with one shock of purple among the forelocks.

"No way... Is...is that Alas Ramus?!"

The mysterious face didn't belong to the little child they'd come to know. Her features had matured up to around Acieth's age—but it'd only been a month since Emeralda had last seen Alas Ramus. This wasn't natural aging at all.

"Is this because of their 'family'?"

"The day after Maou moved in, Alas Ramus slept in late and Maou left for work before she woke up. Then, as Yusa put it, she just grew. That was the first time I heard her talk about living together."

"No way..."

"They'll probably just catch a taxi home now, I think. What happens next is, after the three of them stay together for about half an hour, she suddenly goes back into a 'fusion' state with Yusa's body, and then she's her usual self again."

"...Is that even possible?"

"I guess it is, isn't it? And I'm not with them all the time, so I don't know all the details. But apparently, even if Maou and Yusa go their separate ways in the grocery store, that'll be enough for her to pop out."

"...Emilia and Alas Ramus are supposed to be our key weapons against heaven. Doesn't that mean she's out of their control?"

"Hmm... I guess so, huh?"

Chiho sounded indecisive about it, but this was clearly out of line for Alas Ramus's behavior. It shocked both Emeralda and Sariel.

"If Acieth grew up, there's no reason Alas Ramus can't, after all. But between this and the way the Shiba family is acting, something weird is going on. I mean, Alas Ramus aged several years in the course of a day, just like Acieth can now eat hundreds of rice balls a day. If this is the Sephirah going out of control..."

"..."

"The only reason we're invading heaven is to bring the smile back to Alas Ramus's face. But if something happens to her, it'll make everything we've been doing go to waste. Maou and Yusa won't even want to think about peace on Ente Isla after that. So…whatever they do, they can't do anything to unbalance her. And if the summit fails and all the other Sephirah children are left unhappy…"

Emeralda nervously swallowed. Even Sariel was waiting for the next words out of Chiho's mouth. But:

"…Ente Isla is going to face a serious food shortage."

""Huh?""

"I mean, can anyone really tell you that Acieth's appetite won't get any worse than her last peak? There's a nonzero chance that she'll grow into this huge monster gobbling up wheat fields, isn't there?"

Chiho was deadly serious. It made the smile come back to Emeralda's face. "The scary part is that it doesn't sound like a joke."

"I'm being serious here," Chiho pouted. "…Ah."

As they spoke, another change occurred to Alas Ramus. Her whole body faintly glowed, Maou and Yusa working together to pull her back into the alley. Half a minute later, out came Emi—carrying the baby Alas Ramus in her arms like always—and an exhausted-looking Maou.

"The police would definitely misinterpret this if they saw it, wouldn't they?"

"That's why this is so much trouble… Oh, they got a taxi."

Seeing how disconcerted Maou was, Emi hailed a cab, letting him climb in first before following behind. The trailing trio watched the car go, giving one another convinced nods.

"Look…I don't care what you do, but quit messing around with my life and my SFC, all right?"

"All I can promise is that we'll try our best."

"But…now I'm really glad I came to see you, Chiho… I'm glad I forced myself in, in a way."

Eyeing his surroundings before removing the dimensional barrier, Sariel waved and began to head home, as Emeralda placed Chiho on her back and flew upward.

"Sariel! Thank you for joining us!"

"Farewell for nowww!"

Sariel looked up at them and shrugged.

"If they shout at me like that, what're they gonna do if somebody notices?"

But for a change, his face was meek, unironic, without his trademark sneer.

"So, Emeralda…"

"Yesss?"

"You brought me around the whole city after I got home from exam prep, so can I ask a favor of you, too?"

"…I have a feeling it's gonna be a biiig one," she chuckled, as Chiho whispered something into her ear. Chiho's house was straight ahead, but Emeralda looked back at her, astonished, like she had heard something unbelievable.

"Look in front of you, please."

"Are, are you serious, Chihooo?"

"I am. Like, so serious, even *I'm* surprised. It's weird to say, but Suzuno is the one who led me to be this way."

"Oh… You mean her approaching the Devil Kiiing?"

"Right. So that's one more reason why I'd like Maou and Yusa to remain where they are for now."

"…What a meeean woman you are."

"I'm putting 'Chi' behind me."

After they landed at her doorstep, Chiho turned toward Emeralda, hands on her hips. The two were little different in stature, but to Emeralda, this otherworldly girl now seemed like a giant. That's how much sheer ambition there was to her body and expression.

"I'm going to do it, Emeralda. A regular teenage girl, with no fighting power or experience in life, is going to create an Ente Isla where nobody, human or demon, has to lose their life. So…"

Could I reach that place full of smiles?

Emeralda asked herself the question for a moment, then quickly found the answer. There was no way she could. Even if she was born into the exact same position Chiho was, she doubted she could do it. But after hearing the plan she had going, Emeralda thought that maybe, just maybe, Chiho had a shot at it.

"So Emeralda, whatever you know is fine. Tell me *everything*, from your angle. It's bound to be different from what Lidem told me. Otherwise, I'm not giving you any rest tonight."

"...Sleepless nights are bad for your heaaalth, you know."

"I'm fine. I'm not even twenty yet."

"...You really haaave become an uppity woman, haven't you?"

From Emeralda, it sounded like a compliment. Chiho gave it an ironic grin.

"That's thanks to everyone around me."

✳

Placing the fast-asleep Alas Ramus in bed, Emi kneeled down on the floor, exhausted.

"Hey, you all right?" Maou called out to her.

Emi just shook her head, face buried in the surface of the bed.

"...Nmm."

He didn't say anything else.

Having Emeralda ambush them after work was enough of a surprise, but then she'd prodded their most sensitive areas and voiced her clear disapproval of their living arrangement. Looking back, Maou knew nothing about the pasts of Emi's friends. He was aware of Emeralda's and Albert's birthplaces, but that was about it—he didn't need anything else.

Still, after everything she said, Maou really had nothing to fire back with, and Emi must've been just as bewildered. Emeralda wasn't really the type to place her own needs first in a scenario like this—that must be how much weight Emi's presence had in her heart. Emi and Nord hadn't talked about it lately, and of course Suzuno was acting strangely, so he had forgotten all about the past—but it was a long-overdue reminder of just how much the people of Ente Isla hated his guts.

"...Well, this ain't good. It ain't good at all."

Lately, he had thought he was surrounded by people who understood him. Wurs, Rumack, and other people in those positions weren't forgiving him, but they were willing to accept his actions as belonging to the past—or so he thought.

"But... Yeah."

Maou looked at Emi in the dark bedroom, now fully downed, Alas Ramus sleeping without a care in the world in front of her. It made him frown. He recalled the time when Alas Ramus disappeared for a few days during their struggle against Gabriel, and how much it made him feel like a shell of his former self. It made him wonder why he was arrogant enough to think Emeralda and the rest had accepted his presence among them.

"...I'm hungry."

Maou was in the now-familiar kitchen, turning on the light by the sink and opening the refrigerator.

"Oh, did I eat that?"

He looked around, noticing something missing.

"Hmm?"

"...You looking for the corn?"

"Huh?"

"The leftover corn from the Happiness Set you brought home yesterday."

Over the door he spotted Emi, dark rings around her eyes and hair that looked like she had been in bed all night. She was wrangling with it as she exited the bedroom. It was too dark to see what she was wearing.

"I'm sorry. I used it in Alas Ramus's breakfast this morning."

Come to think of it, there *were* some rolled-up eggs with corn in them on the table earlier.

"Oh, that's what that was?"

"I had less left than I thought I did. You're hungry, right? There's some fried rice in the freezer you can heat up in the microwave."

"Ah. Thanks."

"I'll use the bath first, so..."

Emi walked across the dark living room, face turned away.

"..."

Feeling an inscrutable discomfort, Maou took a flat dish from the cabinet and fished out a bag labeled SHRIMP FRIED RICE – BARGAIN PACK from the freezer, pouring some out on a dish. After two and a half minutes in the microwave, he took it out. This microwave was supposed to be better than Suzuno's, but the electronic beeping when it was done seemed to last an inordinately long time. He had inadvertently awoken Alas Ramus with it once, inviting Emi's ire upon him.

"Ugghh..."

Hesitant to turn on the living-room lights, he hunched over the kitchen counter and silently began to eat.

"Huh. This is pretty good."

Emi relied on frozen food quite a bit—not that it mattered, but he never saw Ashiya or Suzuno use it much, so seeing it occupy more of his diet was a novel experience. Just over a week had passed since he'd moved in, and generally Emi handled all food prep work. She was good at it, and she told him not to mess with the pantry or cooking utensils unless he had to, so he had left all of that to her.

"...Phew."

There wound up being a lot less fried rice than he'd anticipated from the frozen bag, but it satisfied him well enough.

"..."

So he washed the plate and spoon, placed them in the drying rack, and—having nothing better to do—sat on the living-room sofa. Occasionally he heard shower sounds from the bathroom; on his other side, Alas Ramus would occasionally roll over or mumble something in her sleep.

"Sure is quiet... Hmm?"

Then it happened. There was a dull thud in the bedroom. Maou got up, only to find Alas Ramus now standing on Emi's futon, blearily looking around the dark room. She quickly found Maou, and then began crying like a spilled glass of water.

"Daddyyyyy...! *Aaaahhhhhh...!*"

"Oh, no, did you fall off the bed?"

Maou stepped into the bedroom, reaching out with both hands to pick up the sobbing child.

"Weeehhhhhh... Owwwwww..."

"There, there... That surprised you, didn't it?"

"Waaaahhh...!"

Listening to the heavy, piercing crying, Maou returned Alas Ramus to bed, then lay down next to her. Still startled, she put her arms around his neck as she sobbed...but after about five minutes, she finally fell silent. Maou attempted to move, but Alas Ramus reflexively tightened her grip on him, so she must not have been asleep yet. It looked like he'd be stuck for a while, but Maou was tired, too, almost ready to conk out with the little girl's hands around him.

"...Everything okay?"

Emi's voice came from the doorway, jarring Maou awake.

"...I think she fell off. She's fine now."

"Oh... Thank you."

"You can relax in the bath a while longer. You're still exhausted, aren't you?"

Alas Ramus's death grip prevented him from turning toward her, but based on the timing, he imagined the crying must've made her hurry to the bedroom.

"It's fine. I'm used to it. Let me dry my hair a little."

"Sure."

He could feel Emi go away. Then he heard the buzz of the hair dryer. As Emi dried her long hair, Alas Ramus—finally fast asleep—loosened her grip on Maou, allowing him to slowly get up. He ventured to the bathroom, knocking lightly on the door.

"Oh, are you good?" Emi asked, sticking her head out the door.

Maou nodded. "Yeah, she's sleeping now. Does she fall off a lot?"

"What?"

Emi must not have heard him over the dryer's drone. She opened the door fully.

"No, I mean, it's the first time since I came here, so... You don't have her sleep on the floor with you?"

"I did at first, but..."

As Emi explained, she had Alas Ramus sleep on a futon originally, fearing her falling out of a bed, but she kept rolling around endlessly on the floor.

"That's fine in summer, but she'll get a cold doing that in the winter, you know? But if you put a comforter over her in bed, she usually stops at the edge."

"Can you sleep with her inside you...?"

"You should know, having Acieth and all. I'd get woken up all the time. And if you suddenly have someone crying in your brain waking you, it's terrible for your heart. You wanna use the bath?"

"Yeah...I do. I mean, I don't really wanna right now, but it beats bathing in the morning."

Once Emi was done drying her hair, she and Maou traded places, bringing in his sleepwear to shower in the once-strange environment. No longer was he confusing the shampoo with the body soap, and he was now a pro at working the gas valve to get hot water.

Drying his hair and brushing his teeth, he went back outside, finding Emi already retired to the bedroom.

"Did you brush your teeth?"

"Yeah, before I went in the bath."

"Oh."

They settled into their futons, backs turned to each other.

"Men have it so nice, huh?" Emi said out of nowhere. "They can dry their hair so fast."

To Maou, it was pretty obvious why.

"Well, why don't you cut your hair short?"

"..."

A pause.

"Don't make it sound *that* easy. Do you know how many years it took to grow it this long?"

"That's one thing about women I'll never get."

This aimless conversation continued in the darkened bedroom for a little while longer.

"...Are you asleep?" Emi asked softly after a bout of silence.

"...I was about to be."

"Oh, I'm sorry..."

"It's fine. What is it?"

"..."

"You woke me up to say nothing?"

"It's hard to talk about."

"Is it about Emeralda?"

"Yeah... Kind of. I never thought Eme would say all that..."

"It's nothing you have to get out of sorts about. None of it was unfair, really. And she doesn't really think you've forgiven me."

"..."

"But all she did was come over to gripe about how she can't put up with us," he continued. "If I made them all hate me, there's not much I can do now, so whatever, but...yeah."

"Devil King?"

They had never expressly spoken about it, but ever since Maou moved in, they'd slept with their backs to each other. Now, though, Maou rolled over on his other side, facing Emi, who turned her head to look at him but didn't otherwise move.

"You know, if you want to consider your friends' needs first... I mean, I'm actually pretty prepared for that."

"..."

Even with her eyes used to the dark, Emi had trouble reading Maou's face, but she could tell from his voice that he was serious. For some reason, that made her swallow back tears ready to well up in her eyes.

"H-hey," Maou said, surprised.

Emi turned away to stare in the direction of the bed. "You and Eme are both being unfair."

"Hmm?"

"...It's not like I can choose at this point."

It was hard to say just how long Emi let herself feel conflicted before she was able to say that to Maou. Maou couldn't imagine how long, and he had a feeling he shouldn't even try.

"Emeralda really flew off on you, didn't she? Asking you to choose between friendship or a man. Crazy."

"Don't be silly. You'd be surprised how much Eme doesn't know about me."

"Well, that's how it works. You may think you know someone, but for the most part, you really don't."

"Generally speaking, yes. But she really doesn't know at all. I mean…" Emi tensed up, taking a thin, shallow breath. "No matter what happened, there'd never be any way I'd fall in love with you."

Maou's reply was as simple as it was routine. "Yeah, it ain't even worth joking about."

"Watch what you say. We're in front of Alas Ramus."

"*You* should talk." Maou chuckled a bit, then went back to his usual position. "I've actually got an off day tomorrow. I'll watch Alas Ramus, so you take care of the idiots who come visit us at MgRonald."

"…Sure."

"Anyway, good night."

"…Good night."

Maou wriggled around for a little while after, but Emi suddenly sensed him dozing off into a well-regulated snore. She had trouble sleeping, though, her body still clenched up tight. Emeralda, Maou, this family experiment, Alas Ramus, Ente Isla—the future of everything seemed so opaque, nothing she could break through herself. It made her want to scream out of desperation.

"Ahh, I can't sleep!"

She sat up, looking at the serene faces of the two people surrounding her. They were making the exact same face, somehow.

"…What's with that? It's so unfair."

She knew Maou was helping raise Alas Ramus. She regretted inadvertently hurting Emeralda, but she had to commit to this for Alas Ramus. Still, being presented with this formless, silent bond-like thing she and Maou had, it left a bad aftertaste. Was it the way he fundamentally avoided any questions about her and Maou? Or was it some more instinctive discomfort at the fact she was kinder to him than before?

"Hmm..."

She knew her feelings were all over the place. She'd admit that. She definitely accepted the presence of the man Sadao Maou, more so than Satan, the Devil King. She may have been obliged to, but in some ways she even felt an affinity for him—enough so that living together no longer seemed unnatural. But despite that, something was still bothering her about this. She was trying so hard to establish a "family" that she was turning her back on a close friend she had staked her destiny with—but something was still missing in this bond.

Then it happened.

"...Mommy?"

"...Are you up again?"

"Yeh... I gotta go potty..."

The child was sitting up in bed. Not a baby—but Alas Ramus, transformed and looking about the same age as Erone. Normally, she still wore a diaper to bed; there'd be bedwetting issues otherwise. But now she was big enough to be several grades into elementary school, instantly "grown" to the point that she could wake up for bathroom trips.

"Mommy...come with me."

"...All right. Let's go."

It wasn't rare for Alas Ramus to wake up in the middle of the night. For a while, when they began living together, she'd cry through the night in the worst way—but even when she was peaceful, she'd sometimes shout out loud and wake Emi, up to once every three hours or so. But since Maou had moved in, Alas Ramus would wake up almost every day like clockwork at two AM or so—and every time, her physical body would take on another new, and seemingly random, age.

The largest they had seen her was earlier today, on the way home, when she seemed to take on a middle-school age. One time, she'd actually seemed to get even younger than she usually was. She usually reached Erone's age. Emi was used to it now, but she could feel some inscrutable time limit weighing down on them all, impossible to avoid or extend.

"Let's go to sleep now, okay?"

"...Okay."

Emi placed her hand on Alas Ramus's back, much longer than it usually was, and walked back to the bedroom.

"...Alas Ramus?"

"Yeah?"

She got into bed herself—normally, she'd have to be placed there. Emi watched her, smiling a little.

"Good night."

"...Good night, Mommy."

Her slightly matured face settled into a comfortable sleep—and then, little by little, she reverted back to her normal appearance.

"Seeing *this* all the time...you know..."

She wanted to see Alas Ramus's future. She wanted to see her mature for real. The same kinds of emotions any parent would normally have.

Chuckling softly, she gave Alas Ramus's hair a caress, then turned around. Maou was sleeping there, all dopey-faced.

"I think I understand now."

She knew what she was missing, the niggle that had bothered her; the thing that seemed off about this whole "family" thing.

"Come to think of it, I joked about it once, didn't I?"

Emi stood up and took a notebook out from her living room shelf. It was a large, thick book with a plastic cover.

"If we're gonna be a family, there's one thing we've got to have. Don't we, 'Daddy'?"

He couldn't have heard her voice, but for some reason, Maou chose that moment to make a pained groan in his sleep.

✽

Maou spent the next afternoon at Room 201 of Villa Rosa Sasazuka, the first time he had done so in a while. Alas Ramus was napping on the futon set Maou and Emi had purchased for her sleepovers there, the breeze from the window gently stirring around her.

"That was bad of me, wasn't it?"

Maou looked back through a small album. His attention was on a photo of Emi after Alas Ramus had come along; it was taken sometime after summer of the previous year. And the child in that picture shared something in common with the Alas Ramus in front of him, arms above her head as she slept.

"Why didn't I think that was weird at all? It shouldn't even be possible."

In fact, the girl in the photo and the girl in his apartment were exactly the same.

A year was a long time for a baby. It'd bring major changes to her body structure, her face, her height; lots of things. But the Alas Ramus pictured by those familiar with her was always, eternally, the "same as usual."

"I bet you wanna grow up, huh? You want to progress."

People were often a reflection of the astral trends of the world. Maou had interpreted Alas Ramus's and Acieth Alla's out-of-control "incidents" as a kind of rebellion against the stagnation looming over the people of this planet.

As he thought this over, there was the sound of someone unlocking and opening the door.

"I apologize for my lateness, Your Demonic Highness." Ashiya stepped inside, carrying a bag from the grocery store.

"No problem. Sorry to bother you when you're busy. It's been a while since I've seen you like that."

"I heard Libicocco had been feeding you an unbalanced diet, so I came back to prepare some meals in advance…and *hopefully* provide him some guidance."

Ashiya, who presumably was running around Ente Isla building relationships between demons and humans, had an important reason for returning to Japan. Maou had called him over directly, stating that he had vital business for him.

"I am afraid I have little time. Could we perhaps discuss this business while I cook?"

"Sure, that's fine. It'll be over real quick, actually, but it's something I need to be physically with you to talk about, so that's why I had you take time out for me."

"I remain your servant, my liege." Ashiya took out his usual apron and set himself up in the kitchen.

"Ahh... That's a reassuring sight, kinda."

"Is it?"

"It really feels like I'm back home, you know?"

"I would prefer if you said that in the Ente Isla Devil's Castle."

Even the listless jibes of Ashiya's replies put Maou's mind at ease. "Is Chi's summit or whatever going well?"

"Most of the members have already traveled to Noza Quartus, under strict secrecy. Bell, Cervantes, and Emeralda are certainly earning their keep. They are having to deceive quite a large number of people at this point."

"Yeah... Once someone gets high up enough, they get bothered about every single little thing, don't they? You start to wonder if they're actually kicking back on their days off or not. It's tough."

"It seems so, yes. But what about you, my liege? I imagine your stay with Emilia is taxing you a great deal."

"...Just to be sure, Amane isn't blabbering all day about us, is she?"

"I have only heard the basics, once Acieth's food consumption became an issue. If it is for Alas Ramus's sake, I can hardly put up a strong resistance to it. And the state of the two Yesods connects directly to all of our problems, in the battle against heaven..."

"I had thought more people would be against it."

"I suppose we are past that point, are we not?"

"What kind of 'point' are we in if it's okay for the Hero and the Devil King to live together?"

"I cannot say." Ashiya kept up his food prep as they spoke.

"Right," Maou continued, "so there's two things I need to talk to you about. First, about Chi."

"Yes?"

"I want to discuss this with Emi and Suzuno, too, as soon as I'm able, but before we head into heaven, why don't we all meet with Chi's mom and apologize to her?"

"...Ah, yes." Ashiya gravely nodded. "Indeed. I believe that is necessary. When we were guiding her around Devil's Castle the other day, I am afraid I lacked sufficient time to accompany Ms. Sasaki's mother. I had to enlist an assistant instead."

"Yeah, we need all six of us together to say sorry to her. You never know if something might happen to one of us in this war."

"Very true. But what if she asks for her husband to be in attendance?"

"I'll worry about that if it comes. We'll agree to whatever conditions she puts up, of course. Besides, I owe Chi's dad a favor."

"Since when was that the case?"

"I've owed him one for a while, actually; I just wasn't aware of it. He's a cop, you know. My landlord and her gang might object to it, but the reputation of the Devil King's Army is at stake, so I want an official occasion where I can bow my head to her."

"What about Urushihara? He has no formal wear."

"...We'll find something for him. We gotta be sincere with this."

"Very well, then. I will put a schedule together. Now, what was the other topic you wanted to discuss?"

"Well...there's something I want to show you, so take a look once you can step away."

Ashiya looked at the small bundle of photocopied paper in Maou's hands. It gave him pause. The lack of vitality in Maou's eyes had alarmed him a bit, but once he wrapped up his prep and set the burners to low, Ashiya washed his hands and sat in front of Maou.

"Now," Maou said, mentally changing gears, "before I show you this, a word of caution."

"Hmm?"

"...Don't make any loud noise, all right? I just put Alas Ramus to sleep."

"...Very well, then."

This made Ashiya even more doubtful, but he picked up the dozen or so sheets of paper and ran his eyes across the first one. And then, instantly:

"......!!!"

His breathing instantly stopped, his whole body convulsing as the color drained from his face.

"Gnh...!"

With every new sheet he turned over, Ashiya's face seemed to turn a new color, like a stoplight or a disco ball. By the time he reached the final page, his eyes were bloodshot and he looked ready to explode.

"Your, your, your, Your Demonic Highness, what... What... What is...!!"

"Yeah, pretty crazy, huh?" Maou replied dryly, in contrast to his conversation partner.

"This is *not* something you can merely sweep away as 'crazy,' my liege!!"

"Keep it down, man."

"How, how could we *ever* tolerate this outrage...!"

"Well, I dunno if it's an outrage... In fact, I get it, pretty much. Is it really 'wrong'?"

"N-no, no, but this... Why *now*, of all times? We are both trying to defeat the same enemy, and this, this, this is nothing less than stabbing us in the back...!"

"Yeah, but if you think about it...I think I've been told this a lot of times, going back. But the way we're related, I just kind of ignored it, and the other side wasn't *that* serious about it. But, you know, having it all laid out for us like this..."

"Is—is there any evidence?! This could all be fabricated..."

"No, I really don't think we have any wiggle room here! She took out everything we weren't involved with."

"This... This is insanity...!! How could this... How could this...!"

"Now you see why I called you over here? So as my chief advisor and head of the household here in Room 201, I wanted to ask your opinion about it."

"............It is impossible."

"Huh?"

"It is impossible."

The agony behind that simple statement could only be described as gut-wrenching.

"It is...simply impossible to delay this."

The anguished reply drained the life force from Maou, who slumped to the tatami-mat floor. Looking to his side, he saw Alas Ramus's peaceful face as she slept.

"Dahh, I knew it. No luck, huh? Not that we could ever do that at a time like this anyway."

"If... If we defaulted on this...we'd make foes out of not just Ente Isla, but everyone in Japan as well... Ugh...damn it all..."

The photocopies were crushed in Ashiya's clenched fist.

"Whoa, whoa..."

"Damn you, Emilia... Pulling this nonsense...while I was gone...!!"

"I *said*, keep it down," Maou said, seizing the crumpled sheets from Ashiya's hand.

On the first page, writing large in Emi's handwriting, were the words "CHILD SUPPORT INVOICE." The rest of the stack contained a bullet-point list of expenditures related to caring for Alas Ramus since Emilia had taken her in last year. Food and clothing were on there, of course. There was even a section devoted to the rent at Urban Heights Eifukucho, although it was a comparatively small amount.

The grand total: 283,538 yen.

"Hey, Daddy? If we're gonna be a family with Alas Ramus, I think there's something we're missing in our lives for that."

Those foreboding words came from Emi over breakfast, their timbre enough to inspire a nameless dread in Maou. Being presented with these documents knocked him half unconscious. Once he was awake again, he made a valiant effort to fight back—but then Emi revealed the ledger she had used to calculate her Alas Ramus–related expenses, as well as receipts for everything, explaining that she didn't invoice for anything that wasn't spent on the child.

"For example, I didn't include anything that I wanted to treat her with, like the Relax-a-Bear stuff, or if we went out to eat somewhere nice. But between the clothes, the consumables, the grocery store bill, the electricity, and so on and so on, that's what it came to."

Maou was charged a quarter of running costs like rent and electricity, but for indispensables like heating in winter and air-conditioning in the summer, that went up to half.

"When you add it all together, it comes to 567,076 yen. But I'm her mother and we were forced to live together through events out of our control, so I'll cover half of that. But…"

The words of the Hero, spoken over the breakfast table through the soft smile of a proud mother and a faithful partner, stabbed into his heart deeper than her Better Half sword ever could.

"After all, isn't money part of the reality of having a family?"

Explaining this whole scene from earlier in the day to Ashiya, Maou could see him emotionally collapse, his face ashen.

"But… But 280,000 yen? That is simply too much…!"

"Well, Emi's not expecting a lump-sum payment. And I did some research before you arrived, but apparently after a divorce, fifty thousand yen is about the going rate for child support payments. Considering she isn't charging interest or anything, I think she's giving us a pretty good deal, actually."

"But you have hardly *married* her, much less divorced!"

"It's too late for that. Didn't you say we couldn't ignore this any longer?"

"I—I did, but…"

It would be easy for Maou to flatly reject Emi's demands. But like he just said, Emi hadn't padded the bill unfairly at all. In fact, Maou was impressed how she'd kept Alas Ramus satisfied with such a frugal budget. If he brushed this off, people would think he didn't have enough affection for the child. His very honesty would be called into question.

The "people" referred to here didn't only mean those closest to Maou and Emi—Chiho, Suzuno, Amane, Shiba, Emeralda, Albert, and the like. It could also spark the disapproval of Kisaki, Iwaki, Kawata, Akiko, and the rest of Shiba's family. And if he did anything to disappoint Chiho and the others right now, the already-fragile position of the Devil King's Army—and, in fact, the demon races in general—could receive a staggering blow. Should someone like Wurs or Emeralda catch word of this, there was no telling what kind of hell he'd have to pay at the summit.

At worst, word could go around that Satan, the Devil King, betrayed the Hero Emilia, and everyone would conclude that demons couldn't be trusted after all. Chief Rajid and the Azure Emperor could drop out, and if they no longer accepted demon immigrants, then Cervantes, who wanted the heavens on his side as a counterweight, would likely step away, too. If he did, then even with Dhin Dhem Wurs on her side, Chiho would become nothing but a powerless teenage girl. Nobody would listen to her; the demons would lose the new homes offered to them; mankind would plunge into a world war on the Central Continent, and everything following the battle against heaven would leave a bad taste in the mouths of everyone involved.

"Well, I had the same thought. So I called you over because I wanted your affirmation."

"This… How could this…? *Ugghhh…* Oh, dear, one minute."

Behind the weepy Ashiya, one of the pots on the oven began to boil over. He hastily got up and turned off the burner.

"But on the other hand, if we accept her terms…maybe that'll help give us an edge in the summit. You have to understand for me, Ashiya…I think I'm going to say yes to this."

"…I…I understand, my liege."

Ashiya's grief seemed to be flowing in waves out from his broad back.

"Your Demonic Highness?"

"Yeah…?"

"…Only now… Only now did this thought occur to me."

"Yeah?"

Ashiya turned his emaciated face toward Maou.

"Our Devil King's Army…was defeated long ago by the Hero, was it not?"

"You're a little late to that party."

Two hundred and eighty thousand Japanese yen wasn't exactly cheap, but it was nothing they couldn't work out some kind of payment plan for. A twentysomething worker could earn that in a month after taxes, depending on his position. The issue was that the Devil's Castle inhabitants needed to assemble this 280,000 yen within Japan, using nothing but legal means. They could never use anything they'd seized during their Ente Isla invasion work. Two of the Devil King's generals had dueled against the Hero Emilia and lost…but now, once and for all, Maou was cornered without an escape route.

"I've got nowhere to run."

"No…"

"If I do, we really *will* lose everything this time."

"Yes…"

"Sometimes, you have to put it all on the line. We need to lay low for now."

"I feel we have been laying low for quite a while now…"

"Didn't you say it, long ago? Where there's life, there's hope. We have things we need to do, and to do them, we have to overcome this."

"…Yes. You are right… So money is stronger than a holy sword itself…"

At that very moment, the Devil King Satan and Great Demon General Alciel felt, deep down, for the first time, that the Hero Emilia had well and truly defeated them.

"First, I'm gonna grovel to Emi and ask her to wait a bit on repayment. If I can just give her a hundred or a thousand yen from my salary a month, that ought to tide her over for the time being. In the meantime, do whatever you need to survive the summit and make the Azure Emperor agree to take in demons first."

"D-do you think that is possible? Ms. Sasaki has declared that she will chair the summit fairly and without favor... Your Demonic Highness, do you actually think living with Emilia has hurt your standing with Ms. Sasaki?"

"Ahh...maybe."

"Why *now*, of all times?!"

"It's not my fault!"

"My liege, your face tells me you know the reason for it!"

"No, um, I know she wants to keep it fair, but we're all busy people, right? I don't think Chi is actively out to get me or anything. And we're at the point where if we delay this any further, the human factions are gonna start gunning for each other."

"That is so calculating of you! Failing to hide that would be the most foolish of approaches!"

"Look, you don't even get why Emi and I kicked off this summit in the first place—even though you and Chi are the guys who planned it out! Can't you help steer this at all?! You talked about invading Devil's Castle one more time, but what's that stuff even about, anyway?! I thought we were invading heaven to keep from seeing any more human and demon casualties!"

"That is the direction we are aiming for, yes! If Cervantes can be brought to our side, that would improve our chances of success, but we also need to address everyone's postwar interests—including those of our Devil King's Army! That, if anything, is the main topic of discussion!"

"C-can Chi even *do* that?! That hobbling old hag's just gonna make her do whatever she wants!"

"I—I intend to work against that happening, but it is difficult to contact Ms. Sasaki over there...!"

"Well, *you're* not controlling Chi at all either, then!"

And in the midst of squabbling, the doorbell to Room 201 rang. A voice shot across the silenced apartment.

"Hello? Maou? Are you here?"

"Chi..."

It was Chiho's voice. She didn't need to ask. Their voices were easily heard from the walkway outside.

"The... The door is open," Ashiya managed to blurt out.

"All right," she said in her usual voice as she came in, like everything was normal.

"H-hey, Chi."

"Good afternoon, Maou...and you, too, Ashiya."

"H-hello..."

"Wh-what's up, Chi? This is kinda sudden..."

Maou and Ashiya could feel an enigmatic force exude from Chiho's body. Really, though, she was the same as always. The only difference was that Maou and Ashiya were beginning to feel pangs of fear in her presence. That was how much Chiho had accomplished in such a short time.

"Well, I wanted to ask you a favor..."

"A-a favor?"

"Yes. Something important for the invasion of heaven. It looks like the things we're keeping at bay in Ente Isla won't hold for much longer, so I thought maybe it was time to get things moving."

What was this teenage girl talking about? She had only just turned seventeen, and now she was making a Devil King and Great Demon General bend to her will.

"I received word from Lidem Wurs that Rumack and Cervantes worked out their schedule. I know it's a bit hurried, but the summit's set to begin two days from now."

She looked straight at Maou, as carefree as a manager hastily putting together a professional sports team.

"Maou?"

"Y-yeah?"

"I need you to choose."

"Choose...?"

Was she going to pick *this* moment to make him choose between herself and Suzuno? The thought raced across Maou's mind. He didn't expect what came next.

"What do you like in miso soup—radish, or tofu?"

"............What?"

A total mystery. Maou had no idea what Chiho was getting at. But she just smiled back at him.

"Your choice could change the summit, and with that, the future of Ente Isla. So…choose carefully for me, okay, Maou?"

Three days after the teenager asked the King of All Demons about his preference in miso soup…

◊

The roaring seemed to vibrate the air itself, exciting the hearts of everyone in the area. Faced with the beast's majestic presence, which seemed to extend up to heaven, all who viewed it were rendered powerless. But one person was audacious enough to stand before this towering ancient demon.
"I have to say, getting to see it in motion like this… Whoa!"
"Chief! You are too close!!"
Chief Rajid Rahs Rian of Vashrahma smiled at his hapless attendant.
"Don't be silly! I'll never see this again in my life! I must get as close a view as I—*whooaaaa?!*"
"Do you think I like putting up with your stupid whims—*gahh!*"
The dragon's tyranny gouged deep into the Central Continent, as the great lizard Kinanna awoke and focused its rage upon the Nothung. Rajid himself was at his feet, marveling like a child as he nimbly darted around to avoid being crushed—and unfortunately, both his assistant and Albert had their hands full keeping him safe.

"————!!"

"Ah, the language of the demon realms, isn't it? What is he saying?!"

"Why would *I* know what some addled lizard is saying?! Why the hell aren't the Malebranche ready yet?!"

This was the scene of the "final battle" for the Federated Order of the Five Continents force coming from Saza Quartus, about half a day's journey south of Devil's Castle.

"Well, isn't he going to entertain us a little? I've played along with your big scheme long enough!"

"I'm not willin' to risk my neck for the whims of some fancy leader!"

The rapscallion of a king, all too willing to go right up to Kinanna's feet, made Albert wince.

"What are the Malebranche going to do? We discovered the hard way just how gifted they are in illusory magic. How will they use that to exorcise this lizard?"

"Somehow, I guess! That's what they said they'd mainly use! Apparently different branches of their tribe are better at different types of spells! And the followers of Farlo, Ciriatto, and Libicocco all have slightly different appearances—*aahhhh!!*"

A beamlike wave of magic shot out of Kinanna's mouth, aimed squarely at the screaming Albert and Rajid.

"Wow! There's just no end to his power!"

"Stop admiring him! You sure you can keep this up for a whole week?!"

But just when Albert was about to fully vent his frustrations on the king:

"Al! Chief Rajid! Step back! Ciriatto's forces are ready!"

At Emi's signal, Rajid reluctantly ran a healthy distance away from Kinanna. The other Vashrahman fighters scattered away as well, distracting the lizard and halting his indiscriminate attacks for a moment.

"Whoa!" Standing there, Rajid groaned at the overwhelming demonic force filling the air around him. It weighed down on him more than Kinanna's beams of magic, hitting the humans in the area hard as it swirled around the beast's feet.

"Albert! Chief Rajid! Get back!"

With this demon-magic release, a team of sorcerers in Church garb, led by Emi, stepped between the Vashrahmans and the demonic force, building a barrier of holy force to resist it.

"Ciriatto! Go ahead!"

Once she was sure every human in the area was protected, Emi gave the signal. Kinanna was instantly swallowed by a column of light that seemed to support the sky itself, making him roar in anguish.

"Whoaahhh!"

"Ngh...!"

Even with their overwhelming resistance to demonic force, Emi and Albert were almost felled by the screaming. The column of light shimmered a little.

"Look out!"

But another column, this one a holy barrier, built itself up around the demonic light, supporting it as it extended upward.

"Pretty shoddy magic, huh? Letting way too much energy dissipate. At this rate, all the world's forces here are gonna reconsider things and start comin' our way."

Gabriel was looking as breezy as ever as he used holy magic to "reinforce" the demonic column.

"If you think so, give it your full force! I need you to work harder than all the Malebranche together!"

"Man, what a slave driver..."

With a guileless smile, Gabriel directed his holy force against the demonic barrier built by Ciriatto and the twenty Malebranche serving him. The sheer quantity of his force was just as palpable as Kinanna's own demonic beams.

"So is this really gonna quiet down that lizard?"

"Just see how it turns out! Even before now, the Malebranche had been working with Bell's people undercover, doing exactly this!"

"Huh. …Oh, you're right."

The pillar of demonic force began to shrink within the holy barrier. Inside was Kinanna, miniaturized and only about twice the size of an adult human being.

"But *that's* what it does to the land, huh?"

"There's no way to avoid that."

The Malebranche's magic absorption spell returned the target's demonic force into the ground. Before Kinanna began his rampage, Ciriatto's team had worked under Ashiya and Urushihara's direction to fine-tune the balance of the holy barrier, attempting to ensure that the other four major continental forces detected no power being thrown around besides Kinanna's.

"That's why those sorcerers were able to protect the Vashrahman warriors so quickly, huh?"

"You were here the whole time! Why didn't you know that?"

"Well, I mean, all I got told was to keep him from movin' around, and…y'know, I didn't really care about the other li'l details, mm-kay?"

It was unclear whether he understood just how vital he was to the defense of Devil's Castle, but with Gabriel unleashing his full powers, things were finally starting to go in a good direction—for Emi and her allies, and for the attendees at the summit.

◊

Two days after Emi defended Rajid in battle while grumbling about Gabriel's laziness, Crestia Bell was invited by Dhin Dhem Wurs to a certain favorite restaurant of hers in the Goat Pasture. She was heartily scarfing down a Mongolian barbecue–style meal with Farfarello when an attending cleric flew inside with a handwritten note for her. This attendant was clued in about the invasion of heaven—in fact, he was actually a Saint Aile scientist working under Emeralda, posing as a cleric here.

"It looks like we had nothing to worry about after all."

Receiving the news, Crestia let out a sigh of relief and presented the note to Wurs, still intently focused on the meat cooking in front of her.

"This batch is just about done. Read it to me."

"Right away. ...Ah, I can picture Archbishop Cesar wailing to himself right now..."

The note was likely penned by a Church knight in Cesar's service, one unfamiliar with the heaven plot. It was hastily written, like the trail of a spasmodic worm, and it read:

"'The Azure Emperor himself will be at the negotiation table.'"

"Old man Hu himself, eh? Well, how dutiful of 'im."

The "Crusade" Church force was attempting to invade the Central Continent from the north, but on the east side of the land, Efzahan's Eight Scarves forces were now fully deployed, not even trying to hide their intent to keep these crusaders in check. To the Church forces, who initiated their Crusade with the promise that they'd not engage in any major wars, the idea of confronting the Scarves was a nonstarter. Instead Cesar, an Archbishop and one of the most powerful figures in the Church, figured he could overwhelm them with size and negotiate from there—but Efzahan's response was to send a figure who made Cesar look like small potatoes.

Cesar was no doubt feeling quite cornered and flustered by the Azure Emperor and his knights. And the Emperor's arrival, of course, was all part of Suzuno and Wurs's plan. As the autocratic leader of Efzahan, anything the Emperor said came first—but Cesar was only one of the six Archbishops; he couldn't function as the lone decision-maker for the Church knights and Crusade forces. And if the two sides of a negotiation had completely different powers, it'd be impossible to work out any kind of useful international agreement.

Suzuno, meanwhile, was the supreme commander of the Crusade forces—but she was in the Goat Pasture being "cross-examined" by the leaders of the Northern Island and wasn't available. The remaining three Archbishops were far away in the west—and for *some reason*, Cervantes was facing a mountain of work back at headquarters, so he couldn't answer Cesar's summons. Thus, from the very start, Cesar had nothing to negotiate with. He'd likely return to Welland Isa with little to show for his efforts.

"To be honest with you, I did not expect the Azure Emperor to go this far. When I heard the Jade Scarves were to be deployed, that did concern me for a moment, but..."

But to Suzuno and her allies, the Azure Emperor made no secret of his dreams of world conquest, and with his advanced age, there was no telling what truly lay in his heart. He was a fearsome adversary, and for a long time, it was unclear just how serious he was about participating in the invasion of heaven. But he agreed to join forces with them in the summit, as planned. That seemed to put Crestia's mind at rest, but behind Dhin Dhem Wurs's impressed smile was a burning flame of caution.

"Listen, shrimp, does Alciel have any interest in usurping old man Hu's throne?"

Crestia almost fell out of her chair. "Huh?! Where did *that* come from?!" She shook her head at Wurs. "I find it very unlikely Alciel has any intention of the sort. Not at this point. It would impugn on the whole purpose of the summit, and all it would do is relocate the Devil King's Army to the East. It would do nothing to fulfill their goals."

"...I'm sure it wouldn't. Even *I* know that much. But if so... phewww..."

Wurs took the smoking pipe placed next to her, fished her stash of tobacco leaves from her pocket, and packed some into the bowl.

"I tell you, that crazy old man's gonna cause us some serious trouble after all this. He will..."

◊

Two days after Suzuno and Wurs's barbecue fest:

"Ughhh... The Azure Emperor himselllf?"

"Yes. Apparently Archbishop Cesar's been crying to himself the past two days, cycling between Welland Isa and Noza Quartus over and over."

"Things must be in a paaanic around by now, no?"

"We couldn't ask for a better way to buy us some time, but…"

"But we might paaay for it later."

In Lamoise, the port city in Kierence on the east edge of the Western Island, people and supplies were sailing northward in an incessant flurry of activity to answer Crusade demand. Emeralda and Rumack were watching the port's activity from the Saint Aile diplomatic mission in Lamoise.

"Well, I'd say that if we can work to pay back the favors we owe, then fine. There are many ways to repay them. Is Bell in Phiyenci now?"

Beyond the window Rumack looked through, a large sailing vessel cut across the port, a lone figure traveling eastward among the Crusade ships going north.

"Yes. She said she is being 'reprimaaanded' by Lady Wurs at the moment."

"I'm glad *she's* taking it easy."

"Well, when you reach her posiiition, your mouth stops saying the things you waaant to say. I'm sure that's familiar to you, isn't it, Ruuumack?"

"Sometimes you can, and sometimes you can't. Which… Well, I know Suzuno has no interest in doing anything beneficial for the Church, but as a Great Demon General, she's certainly biding her time. I feel bad for Alciel."

"Ohhh, she can't help it! Besides, Alciel is running roughshod around the worrrld right now for us, in many waaays. Sometimes we just need to go with the flowww."

"…The way Emilia describes it, it's usually other people running roughshod over him."

"Oh, maaaybe, yes…"

As they spoke, another ship ventured off to the east. It was headed for Wezu Quartus, a government hub in the western Central Continent and a city that, by and large, had ceased to function.

"Speaking of Emilia, is that whole issue still ongoing?"

Rumack gave Emeralda a mean-spirited look as she jabbed at her. Emeralda didn't bother to hide her dismay as she brushed Rumack's hand away.

"I can't say I've come to accept it, nooo, but…well, after some more events, I feel a little bit more graaatified about it…so I'm letting it go for nowww."

"You don't have to force it."

"Oh, quiiit it!"

"…But this, too, is something we might have to thank Bell for. The East, North, and South didn't raise their hands, so all the other spoils they stood to gain from the heaven invasion will come to the West…or to us, really."

"You want to push all the tiresome things on Bell and Cervaaantes?"

"Ah, they're used to it. I'm sure they'll agree to it."

"Hopefully sooo, but as you know, neither of them will go down eeeasy, right? They both have their own power…"

"Yes, I know."

Rumack's face didn't change at all. She knew what Emeralda wanted to say, and she had an answer prepared in advance.

"But all these leaders, nations, and lands stepping forward… If we're missing one of them, then nobody's going to survive unblemished. No humans anyway. And they're human, too, right?"

"…Yesss, more or less."

"That much, I can tell from those two I saw in Devil's Castle. In fact, if they're among the higher end, they might be far more tractable than the Azure Emperor or the Devil King's Army."

"Oh, don't let your guaaard down. In Japaaan, I learned, they call that 'triggering an event flag.'"

"I know. But supposing we've already triggered it…" Rumack watched the third ship set off, throwing a kiss at its stern. "That's when the summit and the Devil King's Army take center stage, isn't it?"

"You're a meeean woman, too, Rumack…"

"Am I? I'm normal. I'm the most normal person out of all of us dragged into this battle. Everyone else is such a monster, it makes me tremble."

If she was playing dumb, Emeralda thought, she could at least try to act like it a little more. But there was no point picking on her for it.

"And now someone normal like me is about to reel in this 'angel' from across the sky. Could you even imagine anything scarier?"

"Yes, yes, all riiight…"

Emeralda just rolled her eyes and shrugged.

"And that's exactly why we need Archbishop Cesar to do his best to drag on his talks with the Azure Emperor. Unless he can give us at least another week, that'll just lead to more needless sacrifices."

"You're riiight." Emeralda sighed. "I heard from Chiho about a conflict in a meadow in the northeast Central Continent that caused nearly a hundred caaasualties. The Church knights and Eight Scarves forces are farrr too bloodthirsty for their own good…"

"But even if a hundred people die, the Church and Efzahan can both keep saying they advocate for peace. That'd be unthinkable back before the Devil King's Army appeared. The world's gotten a lot more peaceful, hasn't it?"

"It sure haaas," agreed Emeralda, her eyes distant. "And meeeanwhile, we're cheerfully chatting about it like it's perfectly fiiine."

"We're probably not going to heaven, no. I doubt you'd find heaven anywhere…"

Rumack grinned.

◊

While Emeralda and Rumack shared a chuckle…

"And…*oof!*"

Gabriel swung his broken Durandal sword, neatly slicing off the end of Kinanna's tail. It flew in the air, still a good ten yards wide at its base.

"Whoa! Another lively tail this time!"

"Again, why are you here?! You're leaving yourself wide open!"

Albert once again had to save Rajid from being flattened, this time by a massive tail flying straight for him.

"That's the third time this week! How many tails d'you wanna take home, anyway?!"

"The more, the merrier!"

"Are you insane?!"

It had been a week since the summit, and Rajid's men had gone through a cycle of draining Kinanna's magic force, shrinking him down, waiting for him to rest and almost get back up to size, then shrinking him once he got violent again. Somewhere along the line, Kinanna began emitting light beams from his sharpened tail. Gabriel chopped it off to stop him, and they quickly found that this made him much more susceptible to Ciriatto's magic.

Now he had just done it again for the sixth time, and at this point, the best Kinanna could do was grow not quite as large as a tyrannosaurus.

"I'd like to bring this to an end pretty soon, guys!" Gabriel whined as he looked toward Devil's Castle. "If we go too far and he can't revive himself again, that's kinda trouble for us!"

With the summit behind them, the date of the Devil's Castle launch was rapidly approaching. Repair work, inside and out, was proceeding at a feverish pace. At the heart of this effort was the core inside the castle, the device that the relics of the Devil Overlord Satan would be inserted into; Urushihara was currently fixing that up himself.

"He better not be procrastinating in there, man!"

"Well, supposedly we can launch it now, but the timing's important, and even if he's got his memory back, it's not like that fixed his personality or anything, so be patient, mm-kay?"

"I can only be patient for so long!"

Except for Rajid (who was tense as ever about this great dragon-slaying expedition), the third Kinanna-neutralizing run in a week was starting to tire out most of the people involved in it, even Gabriel.

"The weight the Azure Emperor's placing on Noza Quartus is

about to get lighter. We need to keep it in a launchable state at all times, or else Bell and the Scarves won't hold out afterward."

With this battle, nothing would truly start until the invasion of heaven began. Right now, though, Devil's Castle was poised to fly back to the demon realms, and whether they launched it or not, they couldn't wait very long for the kind of "angelic descent" the Western Island would be convinced by. The people from the West could blow up if their Crusade posted no results, and if they did, the flames would spread to the East and North as well. If they wanted to keep the death and sacrifices to a minimum after launching off the Central Continent, they had at most a month to invade heaven and defeat its leader.

"But, y'know…"

Gabriel looked at the skies above Devil's Castle to the north.

"If *he's* got his memories back, let's trust in that guy's secret plan, mm-kay? Lucifer says that if we got whatever Kinanna was guarding underground in the demon realms, invading heaven will be easy. He's the *last* person you'd expect to reveal something like that. Doesn't it make you wanna bet on that dark horse?"

"Well, unlike you people, I've lived a steady life— Whoa!"

Kinanna, restrained by dark magic a sixth time, began to wither before them.

"Great, our quota's done for the day… Hmm?"

But something was different this time. As the tyrannosaurus shrank down, out from the pillar of light came a sort of lizardman, walking on two feet. It was Kinanna's "person" form, last seen over in the demon realms.

<"…It seems the sharpening is over.">

"Hmm?"

"What did he just say?!"

Albert and Rajid stood on guard, confused at this. But with his sharp eyes, not at all like the deranged, violent lizard from before, Kinanna looked deep into the northern sky.

<"Oh, my, and so the great moment is arriving soon?">

"I don't think he's just talking nonsense now. Or is that…?"

Gabriel, the only person on hand who could understand Kinanna without an Idea Link, followed his gaze to the north.

"Ohh?"

He could see Emilia storming ahead at top speed.

"If she's in *that* much of a hurry…maybe this is it, huh?"

Gabriel eased up, relieved in his fatigue, and attempted to heft Durandal on his shoulder—

"Owww!"

"…You do that every time, don't you?"

—and managed to cut his shoulder, T-shirt and all.

◊

Five days ago, Emi had joined Rajid and Gabriel on their wild lizard-tail chase. Today, she was hiding out in a forest north of Devil's Castle with Laila. She was fully outfitted in her Better Half and Cloth of the Dispeller armor.

"I have to say, Archbishop Cesar is much more worldly minded than I thought."

"He's had a much longer career than Cervantes, but he had his position as head taken from him, and now Lady Wurs is treating Bell as much more important than him. I'm sure he doesn't like that. That's why he's impertinent enough to do something like this."

Farfarello, tasked with staying undercover and guarding Wurs in Noza Quartus, yesterday had reported that Cesar was heading for Devil's Castle with a small team of handpicked fighters. Exasperated at the complete lack of progress in his negotiations with the Azure Emperor, he'd taken advantage of Crestia's attention being diverted northward and decided he had to put up *some* kind of result—that's how Farfarello had analyzed it. This, of course, was one potential development they'd fully anticipated—the powers of Cervantes, seeking to block Cesar without leaving his headquarters, had a lot of impact.

"Really, Bell has it the easiest out of us all. She's just sitting there in the North—getting 'yelled at' officially, but I'm sure Wurs is taking her out to lots of meals. I doubt it's a very grueling experience."

"Maybe it looks that way from the outside, but with *that* kind of thing, the more luxurious the surroundings, the harder it is. It's a much nicer meal if you're having handmade pot stickers at home with someone you love instead of three-star French cuisine with someone that gets on your nerves. I'm sure *her* nerves are frazzled by now."

"Right, but that three-star French dinner isn't gonna taste *bad*, is it? I've never tried it, but… Anyway, aren't they gonna be here soon?"

"Yes, they certainly know their stuff."

"They're faster than I thought. That must be how much of a panic Cesar's in."

"They don't want to be found by the Eight Scarves, either. They have their scouts out, supposedly. Just because they know their stuff doesn't mean they want to start killing. Let's get going."

"Can you really do this?"

"I'm pretty decent, actually. I always was good at studying."

Emi and Laila's role was to block the advance of the force Cesar sent out. Stopping them by force would only lead to a second and third attempt from Cesar, so they were taking a stealthier approach. The broad stretch of road they were on, once a vital artery between Noza Quartus and Isla Centurum, still bore the scars of the Devil King's Army and was already about to be consumed by the surrounding forest. There, on one side of it, an astonished Emi looked at Laila's hands.

"Oh… Yeah, you always *were* involved in medicine, Mother…"

"Yes, and I know my way around the demon realms, so I've learned a fair amount about demonic magic…"

The holy magic swirling in Laila's hand produced a second Emi next to the real one.

"…and so, I can replicate quite a bit of the Malebranches' demonic magic with holy force."

"This is so weird."

The illusion conjured by Laila was akin to a live TV camera

pointed at Emi. Any move she made was projected onto a screen of holy magic, making it look like two of her were in perfect sync.

"So I need to stand in front of you and act like an idiot?"

"Well, put some effort into it, please. You need to be Emilia Justina—*divine*. Enough so to make them abandon the orders of a greedy Archbishop."

"All right, but… Alas Ramus?"

With a sigh, she spoke to the child inside of her.

"Hi, Mommy!"

"Promise me you won't come out until I say you can this time, okay? If you can be a good girl, Daddy will play a whole lot with you later."

"Okeh!"

Maou wouldn't appreciate being used as bait like this, but she didn't care right now.

Laila's job here was to simulate a Malebranche illusory spell to project an image of the Hero Emilia to Cesar's advancing force, stopping them in their tracks. They'd have Laila do this instead of a Malebranche sorcerer since building a holy magic–driven screen would make the holiness of Emilia projected onto it less questionable.

"What a farce this is."

"So is everything in this world, nine times out of ten. That's what makes the other ten percent so exciting."

"Yeah, yeah. I pity the poor guys who'll be fooled by a mother-daughter team like *this*."

So Emi "transformed" out of sight.

"…Emilia?"

"What?"

The face of the archangel Laila, as she looked upon her silvery-blue-haired, crimson-eyed daughter, was filled with joy like almost never before.

"I know what you're thinking, all right? Don't say it."

"I'm so happy right now."

And so Emilia's holy magic, along with her image on the holy screen, proved so effective on the spy force sent by Cesar into Isla Centurum that they wasted the remainder of the day chasing that image around the forest.

"Looks like everything's going well."

Deep inside Devil's Castle, Hanzou Urushihara just stared blankly at the machinery he had finished repairing.

"I can't believe everything survived as well as it did. It's sure lucky, or unlucky, or something. But I'm still wondering…"

His speech to himself sounded foreboding, but Urushihara was languidly lying around as usual, his mind on a point far, far up in the sky, far higher than the tip of Devil's Castle.

"They care enough to kill off an Archbishop. They have to be watching all this. Why aren't they reaching out?"

Ever since they resolved to invade heaven, the only real resistance heaven had put up was the assassination of Archbishop Robertio—and by now, Urushihara wasn't even sure that was an assassination at all. There was no evidence either way, but heaven wasn't incompetent—they had to recognize a threat coming their way.

Up to now, they had sent down a constant stream of attackers, from Sariel to Gabriel, Raguel, and Camael. So why, now that the sword was pointed their way, were they not trying to sabotage Devil's Castle?

"Maybe a true freeloader doesn't care what other people think… but I still don't like this."

◊

It was a week before the day of the "resolution"—the day where, for the first time since the Devil King's Army was defeated, the eyes and ears of the world were glued to the Central Continent.

✳

The solemnly-named "summit" was actually a rather cozy affair. The conference room inside the Noza Quartus government building had maybe the same square footage as the first floor of the MgRonald by Hatagaya Station.

There was the Azure Emperor, absolute ruler of the Eastern Island, and his close counsel, the supreme commander of the Inlain Azure Scarves. There was Chief Rajid Rahs Rian, leader of the warrior nation of Vashrahma—the main kingmaker in the Southern Island. There were Cervantes Reberiz and Crestia Bell, two of the six Archbishops who led the largest religion in the world. There were General Hazel Rumack and court sorcerer Emeralda Etuva of the Empire of Saint Aile, the final stronghold of mankind that held firm against the old Devil King's Army long ago. There was Chief Herder Dhin Dhem Wurs, representing all the clans of the Northern Island.

Eight people, each with enough power to annihilate a nation with the twist of a finger, who were now essentially kneeling before a seventeen-year-old girl.

She had given this meeting the honor of being called a summit, but boil it down and it was basically a power struggle among nations, played on a level normal people could never comprehend. Such were the thoughts of everyone here before they took their seats. They were all invited by a chairman from another world, and why would they have such a *literal* outsider tell them what to do? And a seventeen-year-old girl, at that? They could barely keep from bursting out in laughter. She was no warrior, no sorcerer, no demon... What kind of power did *she* have? It was said she was the granddaughter of Chief Herder Dhin Dhem Wurs, but that didn't gibe with her otherworldly origins—there must've been some subterfuge involved.

Nobody could ignore the tumultuous events happening in the Central Continent. But this wasn't a threat on the same level as the advancing Devil King's Army of the past—in fact, this whole thing was nothing more than priming the pump, fulfilling leaders' desires for more land and power. That, of course, was why so much expectation and anticipation were being pointed toward the Central Continent...but the holders of all that anticipation, these people at the pinnacles of human society, were all nervously looking toward the chairman's seat. All, that is, except for Wurs, a light smile on her wrinkled face as she seemed to look forward to how things would turn out.

Their eyes were all looking at the chairman, a girl named Chiho Sasaki. A face quite familiar to some participants, unknown to others. A petite young woman, wearing something called a "school blazer," which was apparently a traditional garment from her own world. Her soft expression and fair skin suggested no kind of intimidation or fighting power at all...but nobody could be careless. That was because Chairman Chiho Sasaki, more than anyone else in the world, was working with the authority of someone far more powerful than herself.

"I believe that everybody here understands the purpose of the Devil King's Army as it wages war against heaven, and that all of you are willing to stake your body and soul on protecting peace and order across the Land of the Holy Cross in the post-heaven world."

This was how Chairman Sasaki began.

"In my homeland of Japan, we have an expression: 'Friends who eat from the same pot.' It can literally mean friends who eat together, but it also refers to people connected so deeply that they will eat and sleep together in pursuit of a common goal."

Was it Cervantes who cleared his throat at that statement? Or was it Rajid?

"I'd like to tell you in advance that I have prepared lunch for all of you today. You will enjoy a meal composed of things people across Japan eat on a regular basis."

The chairman ran her eyes across the attendees.

"And...it is also the same cuisine I eat, 'from the same pot,' with my most cherished of friends. Isn't that right..."

She gave quick glances to the people on both sides of her.

"...Satan, the Devil King, and Emilia, the Hero?"

"...Yeah."

"Yes."

To the right of Chiho Sasaki was the glorious figure of Satan, King

of All Demons, in his original form and large enough that even Rajid—quite a husky man himself—had to look up to see his face. To her left was the Hero Emilia, in her Cloth of the Dispeller and, for some reason, holding a smiling baby.

Everyone in the audience reacted with fear at Satan, then confusion at Emilia's presence. Cervantes, who hadn't participated in the battle against heaven, seemed particularly disturbed. He was the one who stood up, ready to defend himself, the moment the demon and his massive evil force stepped into the chamber. The Azure Scarves commander couldn't hide his own alarm, either—but what struck them as oddest of all was how the chairman, this girl, almost seemed to have the Devil King do her bidding. Normally, unless you had a lot of holy magic, being exposed to the force of a powerful demon would immediately affect your health, even causing death in the worst cases. Meanwhile, here was Chiho Sasaki—no warrior, no sorcerer—and she acted like Satan's demonic aura was nothing to her. It made no sense.

"Now, I've described what we're about to begin as a conference, but in so many words, it's more of my 'request' to all of you. I have listened to a great number of people, and I have used the advice of experts to come up with a 'plan' that ensures none of you will lose anything. Here, I want all of you to be frank with your opinions as we discuss this plan, so we can optimize and execute it more effectively."

"Rather a haughty request, isn't it?"

Rajid was the first to speak. One look from the fighter chief's bearded face would be enough to cow most people, but Chairman Sasaki simply smiled back.

"Yes, it is. After all, if all of you went it alone, you could try till you're blue in the face and never accomplish what's in this plan."

"...!"

"Hee-hee-hee!"

Rajid looked daunted, while Wurs suppressed a chuckle.

"If our Devil King's Army didn't hold this summit," Chiho continued, "the Church's Crusade force would essentially conquer the Central Continent, wouldn't it? And if the Crusaders from Noza

Quartus and Wezu Quartus accomplish their mission... I want to ask Archbishops Cervantes and Crestia this—would you then have these Church forces retreat back to their original parishes?"

"..."

Neither Archbishop was brash enough to reply. The answer was obvious to everyone, but some things are simply better off unsaid.

"Now, Your Majesty the Azure Emperor, if the Crusaders said they 'would meekly go home after completing their mission, so please let them go about their business,' would you believe them?"

"...My forces...in the Eight Scarves...would immediately...resist... with all its might...to protect an independent Centurum from the savages of the West..."

The Azure Emperor, meanwhile, wasn't the sort of leader to hold back his feelings in a place like this. The conference hall immediately grew tense, Cervantes's face stiffening and Rajid snorting derisively.

"Lady Dhin Dhem Wurs," Chiho said. "You have heard the opinions of the West and East, but in this scenario, who would the North side with?"

"Well, we're lending a landing pier to the Church right now, but we ain't got no interest in a war, no. At *my* age, I hardly wanna get in a shoving match with old man Hu here."

"Chief Rajid, General Rumack... As we speak, we already have a conflict involving at least two islands bubbling under the surface. But do the Empire of Saint Aile and Vashrahma intend to make any moves? Because at this rate, we're likely to see one side or the other wield exclusive control of the continent."

"..." Rajid's face turned sour.

"...Hah! Well put." Rumack, on the other hand, smiled like she was enjoying this.

Chiho paid it no mind. "Now, I have an important issue to bring up. Archbishop Cervantes: The battle against heaven the Devil King's Army seeks is, at its heart, an indispensable measure for the continued survival of the human race on Ente Isla. I believe I've already had Archbishop Crestia and Emeralda of Saint Aile inform you as much. With that in mind, I want to ask you: Is it possible to convince Archbishop Cesar, Archbishop Mauro, and all other followers of the Church faith that this is the truth?"

"…That…"

"I'll say in advance that everything I have had you learn about is completely true. If you'd like to see evidence, I can present it to you afterward. That, and Chief Rajid…"

"Mm?"

"Apart from Archbishop Cervantes, everybody in this room is aware of the mission behind the battle against heaven, as well as the fallout—but that knowledge has not been enough to stop their drive to fight it out in the Central Continent. I doubt we will see any suggestions from them about how to stop the conflict…and I can't blame them for that. They all have nations to lead, and once a plan creaks into action, it takes money simply to keep it going. I understand that none of you can pull back at this point, with nothing to show for it. But even with that in mind, the plan I will present you allows all of you to stay involved."

"…Um, what happens if we aren't conviiinced by it? If we refuse to play alooong?" Emeralda asked.

Chiho nodded. "You're free to do that, of course. But…" Then the chairwoman's voice took a darker tone. "…I would suggest that you amply consider who the two people behind me are before speaking."

"What…?!"

"Mmm…"

"*Kah*-hah-hah!"

Rajid and Cervantes turned pale, while Wurs could no longer contain her laughter.

"What kind of story did you *feed* her, Emeralda? This is nothing like the Chiho from before. If it weren't for everyone else in here, I'd think the Devil King was mind-controlling her or something."

"…No, she wasn't the type of girl to say thaaat, or even be *able* to say thaaat. And I don't think the Devil Kiiing can, either."

"…"

The representatives from Saint Aile shared a smile with each other. Satan, within earshot of it, visibly winced.

"Alas Ramus, can you come here a moment?"

"What, Chi-Sis?"

The chairman turned toward Emilia, then took the baby girl from her arms.

"Now, Alas Ramus, who is your daddy?"

"Daddy is Satan!"

A murmur arose in the hall. Satan looked down, hiding his grimace.

"And who's your mommy?"

"Mommy..."

The baby beamed from ear to ear, then pointed straight at her.

"My mommy is Emi-ya!"

The ensuing furor was somewhere between panic and astonishment. Emi, so publicly pinpointed, averted her reddened face, as if holding something back. The emotion behind that blushing was unclear, but depending on how you looked at it, maybe she was being bashful. It certainly lent credence to the declaration of the child in the chairman's hands.

"Satan, Emilia, and I are 'friends who eat from the same pot.' Our battle against heaven began with a drive to make Alas Ramus happy again. So...if you refuse to join this plan, please consider it would be making the Devil King, the Hero, and the entire nation of Japan in my world your enemies."

It caused a major stir, but nobody was able to counter it. It was a wholly irrational line of argument—a threat, really. She was operating on borrowed authority, and she must've known it. But even so, all these leaders, in all their exalted glory, didn't fire back—not even Cervantes, the Devil King Army's greatest enemy.

The chairwoman nodded her approval of the atmosphere around the chamber. Then she turned to the child.

"Thank you, Alas Ramus. Satan?"

"Yeh! Daddy!"

She deliberately gave Alas Ramus back to Satan. This innocent child, trying to climb up the King of Demons as he held her, was the tie binding him and the Hero together—that much was proven now.

"But if you agree to the plan I offer, none of you stand to lose anything. You won't be able to have the entire pie for yourself, but I promise you that you will reap great rewards ahead of the nations that don't participate. Now…Satan?"

"Yeah, yeah… Hey, E…Emilia."

At the chairman's signal, Satan hefted himself up, taking a quick glance at the agitated audience before returning the baby to Emilia. The whole thing was so natural that it only reinforced the strength of their bond—but with that, the cramped-looking Satan left the conference hall. Several minutes later, he was back—this time carrying a large pot, accompanied by a rather bizarre crew.

"A-Alciel…"

One of them was the Great Demon General Alciel, a face many in the audience knew. But behind him, carrying a tray full of small, white globs on little plates, was clearly a human being—and the young girl who followed was even sneaking some bites from her tray as she brought it in.

"Hey, Acieth!" Satan yelled.

"Sorry, sorry! I wait so long, I get hungry!"

The girl Satan called Acieth, upon further examination, seemed to resemble the baby Alas Ramus quite a bit.

"Here, Father, let me help you."

"Father?!"

Those who didn't know Nord Justina had an even bigger surprise after they heard Emilia refer to the human behind Alciel as her father. Soon, though, the hall was filled with an exquisite aroma. Clearly, this was food they had brought in.

"You see, all of you here today are friends eating from the same pot, fighting for Ente Isla's future."

The trays and pots were all lined up on the chairman's desk—then the chairman herself began to lay out place settings for everyone, before their eyes.

"This is an *onigiri*, or rice ball. And this is *tori no kara-age*, a way of frying chicken. This is *myoga no hiyayakko*, a cold cube of tofu with ginger on top, and this is *daikon no misoshiru*, or miso soup with radishes. These are all selections we couldn't do without in the Devil King Army's day-to-day operations. I cooked all of this."

This was the first thing Chairwoman Sasaki—Chiho—suggested to Wurs. She had every intention of harnessing Satan and Emilia's authority for her needs, yes—but she also wanted them to understand the differences between this world and Japan. So, just this once, she wanted them to sample the type of cuisine Chiho and the rest ate at Room 201 of Villa Rosa Sasazuka…and this was the result.

Now, just as Archbishop Crestia, Emeralda Etuva, and Dhin Dhem Wurs were about to dive into lunch:

"No!"

The baby in Emilia's arms stopped them, eliciting shivers from the audience. Facing them, the daughter of the Devil King and Hero sternly lectured them.

"You hafta say 'thank you' first!"

Normally such a sincere order from a toddler would elicit laughs. But the group in here had no idea how to react, simply nodding vaguely at each other.

And then…

THE DEVIL IS TAKEN BY SURPRISE

The participants in the summit all solemnly carried out their parts of the plan.

Rajid had already taken the six tails he'd sliced off Kinanna back to his victory parade in Saza Quartus, calling them "dragon's tails" and presenting them as proof he had slayed the evil infesting the Central Continent.

Just as rumors about the great and honorable feats of Vashrahma and the southern Federated Order were spreading worldwide, the Church Crusade and Eight Scarves armies agreed to send token forces from the North and East to Isla Centurum, promising each other they would avoid war.

As they did, they were greeted by a constant barrage of "miracles" and "nightmares," ultimately forced to flee to Noza and Ea Quartus before even reaching Isla Centurum. The most common sight was an image of Emilia the Hero, followed by the back of an angel and the ghosts of Isla Centurum natives killed by the Devil King's Army. That last one was the product of illusory magic and necromancy, both Malebranche specialties. Between this and the "dragons" Vashrahma vanquished, fearsome rumors began to spread not only among the knights stationed in the Central Continent, but all over the world.

Taking advantage of these rumors, the Eight Scarves began to gradually shift toward allowing the Church knights to advance their soldiers. Not completely, however—in the end, an impromptu "expedition team" was formed to examine these rumors, a combined effort from the Church and Efzahan.

Vashrahma, meanwhile, basked in the honor of arriving first, coupled with the honor of defeating the giant demonic dragons that lurked around. They had demonstrated the threat the Continent posed, and now, the Church and Eight Scarves forces were joining hands to root it out—with, of course, the support of the Mountain Corps and General Rumack's Federated Order.

In essence, this meant the Crusade could continue, but thanks to their agreement with the Eight Scarves, they had to spread their forces across a broad swath of land, making it all but impossible to colonize the Continent and make it look like a mercy mission. The same could be said of Efzahan's forces as well, and the Order and the Mountain Corps acted as intermediaries between them, professing neutrality.

So, while everybody was in this state of not pushing their own ambitions too much, the Devil King's Army planned to launch their castle. They'd have the eyes and ears of the world on them, and all the knights deployed from every corner of Ente Isla would get to witness the moment, rendering them further unable to seize the island for themselves.

Of course, after the battle against heaven was over, the leaders of all these factions would receive a vast amount of helpful information and personnel for their own international and political needs. This included an influx of demon immigrants—a program Efzahan, Phiyenci, and Vashrahma had been expecting from before—but there was also something else, something Cervantes, the Church, and the entire Western Island were willing to give up conquering the Central Continent to obtain.

※

"I gotta say, that was a blind spot for me."

The short summit schedule was behind them. After the world leaders filed out of the conference hall, Sadao Maou—dressed in a T-shirt and shorts that didn't match the room's ambience at all—was groaning.

"Or, like, we didn't think about it much, huh? Or at all, really?"

Emi, Alas Ramus in hand, was in a similar mood. "Well, we weren't talking about annihilating them all at the start. Beyond that, I didn't really care what happened."

"Me neither. But having it all put together like this... It's heavy."

The stack of papers wasn't very big. But now it held the signatures of every participant in the summit. It was a world summit, one the world might never learn of, and in it they had made their final decisions about the heaven invasion.

"So..."

Chiho, the chairman and only member of the summit still in the hall, sat slumped at her desk, looking uncharacteristically exhausted.

"So now we have a date for the Devil's Castle launch, but is it gonna be all right, you guys?"

"All right or not, we gotta do it," Maou gravely said, twirling around a slightly fancy ballpoint pen he'd purchased for his Mg-Ronald managerial exam. "It'll help a lot more to keep our promise than to have the Devil King and Hero not sign this thing."

The record of proceedings for this summit contained the signatures of all the participants, as well as those of three witnesses: Satan Jacob, aka Sadao Maou; Emilia Justina, aka Emi Yusa; and then some kind of scribbly chicken scratch underneath them. That one was written by the one person in attendance the audience was unlikely to forget anytime soon—the name of Alas Ramus, child of the Devil King and Hero.

"No, we're certainly not powerless enough to let Chiho's and the others' names go to waste. It puts even more on our plate, but..."

"My shifts are pretty rough as it is, so I don't wanna take too much time off. It's mean to Ms. Iwaki."

"Well, have Libicocco work hard for a while, and once you're free, you can work shifts for a month straight or something. Ms. Iwaki understands, and so does everyone else. That's one side effect from Chiho revealing it all, huh?"

"One month with no breaks ain't a joke," he snapped before turning to Chiho. "But great job, Chi. I had no idea what to expect when you first suggested it, but it really did turn out okay."

Chiho lifted her face up from the desk to stare at him. "…Well, I tried. I'm still doing all this in between school and exam prep, and I was also going around gathering info without Lidem's help. In my spare time, I was also training to have the holy force in my Yesod fragment sync up so it could cancel out your demonic force, so it was really tiring. And you're making me do all this during exam season, you know, so you guys better work hard, too, okay?"

"Y-yeah. I'm really sorry. But wow, Chi…you were, like, totally different from usual, or…like, using all this difficult vocabulary and stuff…"

"You're right! I was just standing there, but you were flooring me…," Emi said.

"I tried really hard."

""Huh?""

Chiho's eyes were moist. Even now, she was overwhelming the two of them.

"I asked my friend in the student council to teach me how to organize a conference. We talked about model governments, group discussions, that kind of thing," she explained. "With all the meetings we had, I wound up treating him to about ten-thousand-yen worth of food at the diner."

"Oh…"

"I also recorded the proceedings of the National Diet on TV and watched them every day. Mom knew what I was up to so she didn't say anything, but Dad gave me a few weird looks."

"He did…?"

"I even studied how to write up documents like that, because I said there'd be an essay section to the exams. I read three books about business meetings and three other ones on how useless business meetings were. They cost six thousand yen."

"''''…''''"

"But I was still way too anxious, so I had Ms. Shiba and Amane edit and check my script for the proceedings. By the way, you, Suzuno, and Laila need to add an extra ten percent to your rent this month."

"Whaaa?!"

Maou looked at Emi, looking for an out from that final fact Chiho revealed. But Emi was too astonished by Chiho's behind-the-scenes effort to look back at him.

"So I'm really…really tired. I had to say a lot of things to people I didn't want to; I had to act really strong to them. And it was important to keep things fair and secret with this, so I couldn't really talk about any of the important parts with you guys, or Suzuno or Ashiya or Emeralda—and Urushihara's actually working hard for a change, so I didn't want to bother him."

"''''……''''"

Once Chiho was done, she let out a light sigh, then put her face back down on her desk.

Maou and Emi exchanged a glance. It must've been scary for Chiho. Nerve-racking. Even now, she couldn't shed her anxiety, no doubt. As responsible as she was, she had no choice but to go all the way on this. But unlike the *zirga*, where everything she did was rated on a point system, the only way to evaluate how a conference went was to just sort of read the room.

Despite it all, all these power brokers in Ente Isla had just entrusted their futures to a powerless girl from another world. Maou and Emi suddenly felt intensely guilty. They thought their presence had helped support her, but they wound up making her conduct the conference all by herself.

"C'mon, Chi-Sis!"

Perhaps detecting this anxiety, Alas Ramus jumped out from Emi's arms and lifted her hand way up, rubbing Chiho's back.

"…Mmm, thank you, Alas Ramus…but I really am tired…"

Maou stood up at this painful sight. He felt a sudden urge to apologize for his cowardice. "H-hey... Chi... Um, I'm sorry. We..."

Demon or human, it didn't matter here. As someone who came from this world to Japan, he felt the need to apologize for all the cowardice in Ente Isla. It was his way of taking the punishment for making this girl from another planet take up the cross of this world.

"Hmm?"

But then he yelped as he felt something gripping his wrist along the desk.

"Maou?"

Chiho, grabbing his wrist, looked utterly spent. But there was still a daring smile on her face as she looked up at him.

"Reward me."

"R-reward?"

"Yes."

Maou hurriedly tried to adjust his position, but for some reason, Chiho wouldn't let go of his wrist.

"For this job, I'd say Great Demon General Chiho Sasaki worked the hardest out of all of us. Even if you take off points for me causing that furor at MgRonald, I don't think it'd kill the Devil King to offer a reward of some kind."

"Uh... Umm, well, certainly, all this work you did, behind the scenes and stuff... I'm really amazed, so I want to repay that in kind... Umm, what do you want?"

"Yusa, do you think we got everyone on board pretty well with this meeting today?"

"Huh? Me? W-well, yeah, I think so, but..."

"Then if everything goes fine after this, doesn't it mean I helped take the first step toward saving Ente Isla?"

"I—I can see that..." Emi felt flustered, unable to keep up with Chiho's energy.

"In that case, Maou, I'm not gonna be satisfied with just any old reward."

"H-huh?"

Before, when Farfarello first came to Japan, Chiho had made a similar demand to Maou. At that time, she managed to eat three large slices of this cake with tons of strawberries on it—but Chiho had gone through *much* more this time. And, really, the cost of the reward didn't seem like the important thing here...

"S-so what should I do?" he asked.

"..."

Maou still couldn't leave the desk, his arm all but nailed to it. Then Chiho gave a quick look to Emi.

"Yusa... Alas Ramus..."

"Huh?"

"Yehh?"

"I actually have a workroom upstairs, but I left my bag with my notebook and phone in there. Would you mind getting that for me? It's a dark blue backpack. Can you help, too, Alas Ramus?"

"S-sure. All right."

"Yehh! I kin help!"

"Sorry... Thank you."

"Whoa, Emi...!" Maou said.

Emi, pushed away by Chiho's tension, took this opportunity to pick up Alas Ramus and heave the conference hall. Now Maou was left along with Chiho. He turned toward Chiho again, trembling as he wondered what kind of "reward" she'd ask for without Emi or Ashiya around.

"Hey, Chi..."

But Maou couldn't form the remaining words.

"Chiho, is this your bag? It's not your usual one, so I wasn't sure— Whoa, what's going on?"

Five minutes later, when Emi returned to the chamber, she found Maou sitting on a chair (or more just being supported by it as he draped), staring into space in a complete stupor. Chiho was on her feet, blushing a little, similarly draping herself behind Maou's chair.

"Chi-Sis?"

"...Right, that's the one. Thank you, Yusa. Thank you, Alas Ramus."

"Oh, okay...but what happened to the Devil King?"

Chiho left Maou behind, taking the bag from Emi.

"All right, Maou, I'm going back to Japan today," she said—and then she left the conference room.

"Huh? Hey...Devil King? Chiho's leaving... Chiho?!"

Maou didn't reply, Chiho was leaving the building, and Emi had no idea what to do. For now, she decided to chase Chiho out of the chamber.

Maou, left alone, suddenly leaped up from his seat, only now flying into a panic.

"Wha... Ah, uh... Ahhh?!"

He froze again, unable to parse these recent events.

"Maou?"

He could hear the echoes of Chiho's voice from beyond the fog, bouncing around his ears.

"That's half of it there."

Then he looked at the desk Chiho sat at, as if she were still there. And at that desk, as she kept Maou's arm glued to it, she said this just before Emi returned:

"...The other half, I want from you, Maou."

THE AFTERSTORY

The wet sound of footsteps passing through mud and weeds echoed through the gloomy mist of the forest. There were the sounds of metal scraping against metal, hoofbeats, the occasional whinny or cough. They dissipated into the sky the fog concealed; all anyone could tell was that sunrise would come soon.

They were a force of ten thousand knights, all dressed and armored differently. They consisted of a Church corps bearing the flag of the Crusade; a legion of Inlain Jade and Inlain Crimson Scarves, wearing armbands with their respective colors; a force from the Western Island bearing emblems from the Federated Order; and a few Northern Island Mountain Corps men with their own unique equipment. None of them spoke; their eyes were turned downward, and detectable in their breathing was a tremor unbefitting these large, stout men.

"Behold," someone whispered. The people around him timidly looked up. There they saw the sharpened edge that seemed to stab into the dimly lit sky—the pinnacle of Devil's Castle, the headquarters of the Devil King's Army that had terrorized all of Ente Isla just a few years ago.

Someone gulped nervously, a vivid expression of the fear in everyone's hearts. Each of these knights had their own motivations, their own senses of honor that brought them here. They wanted to exterminate this new threat, this new terror from the Central Continent, and thus they were here. But those who survived the last assault on Devil's Castle, led by Emilia, spoke frankly of the intensity, the cruelty of that struggle—tales that were still related to this day. Some who took part in that were no doubt among the ten thousand here right now.

Every one of them imagined a nightmare ahead, unleashed by countless thousands of demons all at once from the top edge of that mist-shrouded edifice. But…there was nothing. Nothing apart from the lofty precipice of Devil's Castle. The sounds of nature were around them—insects and birds, wild animals sensed among them and heard in the wind. The castle's miasma wasn't fatal to them.

There was nothing. Nothing happened. This, once more, was the world of humans.

The sun edged up from the horizon and extended its warm arms out, as if to support the hearts of the knights as they rejoiced at still being in a human world. But just as a sense of relief reigned over the throng of ten thousand, the warm sun and wind cleared the fog a little.

"…Look at that."

One of them noticed what was amiss, even as the ground seemed to rumble. The knights, relaxing in their relief, were suddenly startled out of their respite.

No one could blame them—what they saw would surprise anyone.

And what they saw was that the enormous Devil's Castle, all but piercing into the sky, was now shaking from top to bottom.

In an instant, the sun cleared out the mist, revealing the majestic castle on the other side of the veil. The sight scared the ten thousand out of their wits.

Smoke poured out from the base of the castle, shaking the ground—and in another moment, the edifice itself began to rise up. The performance shook the heavens, the earth, and the petrified souls of all who saw it. In the midst of it, a divine light as bright as the sun itself shot out from the top, transfixing everyone in the expedition team.

It's the Hero, someone said. *Emilia. Is it an illusion? It's her. I've seen her before. That's no illusion.*

"The Hero Emilia!!"

"Brave knights of the world, gathered in the Central Continent!!"

Emilia's voice beat powerfully, convincingly, against the eardrums of all on the ground. The voice of the young Hero who'd once saved the world came equally loudly to all ten thousand of them.

"From this moment forward, the battle moves on to the divine realm. I command you to tell the world! The Devil King has penetrated into the heavens, attempting to make good his escape. But I will never let him flee! Please, all of you, watch as I do battle! May the world be united in peace, and may a new evil never be born bin...ah, be born in this world!"

The fact she tripped over herself a bit in the end was a petty trifle compared to the sight before them. Out of all ten thousand fighters who heard her speech, only one thought to laugh at that stumble. All anyone else could do was watch as Devil's Castle propelled itself upward, sucked into the sky.

"I am Emilia the Hero! And no matter how the world may change, that alone shall remain ever true!!"

With that clarion call, the girl with red eyes and silvery blue hair, surrounded by holy force, raised her right arm high. The Better Half was in her hand, a name even now whispered among the knights—the sword of the Hero, one whose holy force had smitten armies of demons.

"Devil King! Prepare to die!!"

"............................Wow, cool, Mommy........."

The light of the Hero now chased after Devil's Castle as it ascended upward—and in the face of that roaring, that shocking sight before them, nobody was going to remember the faint voice of a little girl that was mixed in. All they could do was stand and gape at the true-blue miracle that just occurred before them.

"...Brave men guided by God! We have just witnessed a miracle!"

The strong voice brought the crowd back to reality. Just one person out of them—the one who noticed the Hero's slip of the tongue and almost burst out laughing—sent her mount forward, robes flapping in the air as she made a bold declaration, her voice almost too commanding for her small stature.

"Knights of the world, you have come from different walks of life, uniting your forces together…and now you have witnessed this! Truly, the guh…the guidance of God is upon us!"

The Archbishop leading the expedition team paused for a minute at "guidance of God," wondering if that phrase was getting repeated too much. But she decided to just let the mood of the crowd take her.

"We will not let the Hero Emilia's miracle go to waste! Now! Time for a triumphant return! We must bring this miracle to the world!"

The agitated knights roared their approval—a roar that echoed across Ente Isla. Dawn was now breaking for all mankind, all across the planet, as one among the ten thousand described it with his spear thrust over his head, and the stories that spread worldwide would grow to call it the "Day of the Dawn."

Now, a new morning had come to Ente Isla.

✳

"I'm *sooooooooooo tiiiiiiiiiiiiiired…*"

On the day of the resolution, when Chiho all but escaped back to Japan from the summit, she tossed her bag away and fell into bed, not even bothering to change.

"…The *zirga*…was so much easier…"

Being asked to serve as chairman of a summit in another world was all fine and good, but now she thought this was nothing she could've taken on by herself. Everyone was thinking far too much of her, and Dhin Dhem Wurs was probably worst among them all. Wurs's pressure was one of the main reasons she'd taken the job in the first place.

But even after Ashiya and Farfarello explained things to her, she remained dissatisfied. What would being okay with a bow and arrow have to do with running a high-level conference without any mistakes? Wurs suggested her for different reasons, of course, but

Chiho wasn't made aware of that, and if she was, she wouldn't have believed it anyway. As Wurs put it, she didn't pick her because of her position or abilities—it was strictly her pluck.

"……"

Either way, though, now she was completely hands-off with the invasion of heaven. From now forward, nothing would happen that'd require Chiho's powers to solve.

"Well…I hope this launches Devil's Castle… That just leaves the invasion… The release of the Sephirah… The transfer of all those demons…? Nah, I'm sure Ashiya will lead that front. Not like most demons besides Farlo's tribe would accept me as a Great Demon General anyway… Ah, but aren't they stopping by the demon realms, too? Acieth and Alas Ramus still aren't stable yet. What were we gonna do about that…?"

Her mind was spinning, like she had a fever. Her role in it was over, but she had no capacity to think about her exams today.

"………Maou………"

She had no leeway at all.

"I……have no regrets."

She thought it was a cowardly move. But while she might've been pushed by her pride as a successful chairman, she did what she did with absolute confidence.

"…It's all Maou's fault anyway…"

Lying facedown on the bed, she cursed the image of Maou's face that danced behind her eyelids.

"You keep postponing the problem, so then *this* happens."

Maou looking troubled. Maou looking surprised. In a way, she'd anticipated all of it. That's why, this time, her heart wasn't racing at all.

"Hahhh!!"

Running out of breath, Chiho lifted her head up. Swinging her legs off the bed, she rifled through her bag. She took a small box out from it, opened it, and placed it on her desk. Inside was the ring made from the Yesod fragment. It had come through for her again this time, but thinking about the future, she wasn't sure she could hold on to this forever. This was a Yesod fragment—a part of Alas Ramus and Acieth.

"When I give this back, it really *will* be over, won't it?"

The words surprised her as they escaped her lips. *What* would be over? The war? The fighting between the Devil King and Hero? Or...

"No, it's not gonna be over. That's what the summit was for. It's what the invasion is for."

Once this war ended, holy energy would slowly dissipate from Ente Isla. That spelled the end for the planet's Gate magic. It wouldn't happen instantly, but as time wore on, it'd be harder and harder to travel between planets.

"I don't want this to end...just for me."

Out of all the people who sat around the table in Room 201 of Villa Rosa Sasazuka, Chiho was the only one from Earth. Everyone else's homes were far, far away in space.

"...I'll never let that happen...after how hard I worked."

Alas Ramus and Acieth weren't even from Ente Isla. The angel's feather pen was made from an archangel's feather. If the angels lost their power, would it keep on working?

"No matter what...I'm never...gonna let it end."

In the dimming bedroom, Chiho brought a finger to her lips.

"It's all right. That's not going to happen," someone said.

"Gahh?!" The presence of a third party in the room made her jump into the air. "Huh? Huh, ah, ah, who...?"

"I understand your concern, and it's not gonna be a free ride like before, I don't think. But there are ways."

Chiho was confused. This was her bedroom, but someone knew it belonged to her—someone who should never be in here. It made her feel panicked, even endangered. She reeled back in her bed, back against the wall.

"Wh-wh-what are you doing here, Urushihara?!"

How long had he been there? Hanzou Urushihara was standing right in the middle of Chiho's room.

"I've been here the whole time, duh."

"D-don't lie to me! It was empty when I came in...!"

"No it wasn't. And it's not just when you came in. Really, I've been together with you for months now."

"Urushihara, you really have to stop playing with me... Urushihara?"

That arrogant voice; that way of speaking. His stature; his appearance—it was all exactly how Chiho remembered him. But something was off here. Not even Urushihara would go barging into Chiho's room without warning, would he? And why would he even think to visit in the first place? He barely left his own room...

"Oh, I've been going out lately, y'know. I've been working. But that's not the issue!"

Chiho's mind and mouth stalled on her, before she finally asked the most fundamental of questions.

"You're...Urushihara, right?"

It was definitely his face, his body, his voice. But it didn't seem right—the *atmosphere* was off; that was the only way to put it. He didn't have that sneer on his face, and it seemed like he was being a lot less elusive with his speech. But his clothes were about the same as always. So did Urushihara really illegally sneak into a room that Chiho hadn't even invited Maou into yet?

But as she thought this far, Urushihara winced.

"Dude, that's mean..."

"Huh?"

"...You know...*that*."

"That... Wait, what?!"

Was he reading her mind? If so, this made even less sense.

"Y-you're not angry?"

"No... I mean, this is all weird, isn't it? First off, how'd you know I was reading your mind just now?"

"You kind of *are*, aren't you? I could tell."

"...Oh. Yeah, sorry. Having your mind read ain't gonna surprise you at this point, huh?"

"No, but..."

"Well...yeah, it's about what you imagine. I'm not the shiftless, jobless 'Hanzou Urushihara' you know."

"I don't think *that* poorly of you."

Urushihara, or whoever this was, used "jobless" like it was part of his name. Chiho couldn't help but poke fun at that.

"So what are you…?" she asked.

"Most people are just one complete thing, right? Even if they get split up in the future, this memory from before becomes a record that exists in the world. It lets people become whole again."

"What…?"

"And that's what you did."

"Huh?"

"You made Ente Isla whole. It never would've happened without you."

"Umm…"

"But there's still something that's been split up in that world, and I have to make *that* whole again. But there's this kind of rule, or something, where I show up to whoever made something whole. Thanks to that, I guess I surprised a lot of people on this planet just now."

"Um… Um?"

"Take a look out the window."

Chiho followed his command, opening the curtains.

"Aaaahhh?!"

Seeing the face clinging to the window outside, she fell off the bed.

"…"

"M…Ms. Shiba?!"

The visage of Miki Shiba, landlord at Villa Rosa Sasazuka, was occupying every square inch of the window space. It was a difficult scene to describe, but somehow, Chiho noticed there was someone else floating in the air, in what little else was visible beyond her.

"Huh?"

Squinting, she realized it was a man she didn't know, floating there with a peeved look on his face. But he wasn't alone. Once Chiho opened the curtains fully, Shiba promptly took a step back, revealing a good eleven figures behind her. Clearly they weren't from Japan, but Chiho could immediately tell—they were all Sephirah children. Something about their aura struck a chord in her mind—the same aura as Alas Ramus, Erone, and Acieth, whenever they got excited or emotional.

The children of Earth's Sephirah were in front of Chiho's bedroom, and they were clearly gearing for battle.

Then one of the figures slipped in front of the window.

"Amane…"

"Hey, I'm coming in. Sorry to surprise you, but we need to see that guy."

The usual gregariousness was gone from Amane's voice. Chiho just stepped back, a bit woozy as she opened the way for her.

"Lemme just say, dude, I'm not trying to hurt anything. It's a total coincidence that I'm here. You guys have known for a long time now that there's an Ente Isla Yesod fragment in here."

The thing taking Urushihara's form stood strong, taking a step forward. He must have known they'd come here.

"If it is, it'd be *beyond* an exception," Amane said. "We've been monitoring the Yesod fragments around here, just to be sure we can handle whatever comes up. I thought something had happened to Alas Ramus at first…but it was Chiho, huh?"

The first time Alas Ramus had ventured a decent distance from Emi, it must've been Shiba and her cohorts watching over them.

"Yeah. So I get why the gang's all here like this. But you must've been watching Chiho Sasaki this whole time. You know she never does anything stupid, right? She's incapable of it. Do you really have to threaten her like this?"

"People can change. Nobody knows what the future will hold."

"There's no real point in us arguing over that. *We* don't know what's gonna happen in the next second, either. …And Amane Ohguro, isn't your very existence the result of a future nobody knew about, too?"

"…Mmm, yeah, I suppose."

"It's gonna be fine, okay? For now, that world's gonna be put together. As for whether everything will work out, well…"

The man in Urushihara's form floated over to the path outside that Amane and Shiba created.

"Um, wait!" Chiho called from behind him.

"Hmm?"

"Are you, maybe…?"

"Ahh, I'm not really any different from the guy you're thinking of."

"What?"

After saying that, the man gave her a breezy smile that looked not at all right on Urushihara's face.

"If I want to, I can hole up in my little space as long as I want to."

"Huh?"

"Ha-ha-ha! Anyway, all these scary guys are staring at you, so I better get going. When I meet you again, it'll probably be…"

He pointed straight at Chiho's heart.

"…when the man inside there gives you an answer, I bet."

"Hey…"

He could read her mind. That was okay, really. But *this* was a huge invasion of privacy.

"Sorry, sorry. That was too private," he said. "But you sure went overboard, didn't you?"

"Heeyyyyy!!"

"Hang in there. You got my support—as someone who's touched your soul—right on your finger."

"I can't 'hang in there' any longer!"

In many ways, those were Chiho's honest feelings. Amane must've seen that, because after putting her hands together in apology, she and the rest of Shiba's gang surrounded the man and faded into the sky.

"At this point, I can't hang in there unless I get that half of my reward!"

Her declaration was greeted only by silence.

✸

"Ugh… Why am I even doing this? You guys think I'm your handyman or something?"

With a heavy thump, a pouty Sariel dropped a bag from a nearby grocery store on the tatami-mat floor. A futon had been laid out in the middle of Villa Rosa Sasazuka Room 201, Sadao Maou lying on it and looking at Sariel with a "why *now*?" face.

"…Sorry. Libicocco's working all day today, and everyone else is busy. Put it down there for me… I'll take care of it."

Seeing Maou try to get up made Sariel raise an eyebrow.

"Forget it. Just keep resting. There's a bottle in here, and I don't want you hurting yourself if you fall down with it."

"No, but…"

"It's fine."

He was being rough with him, but behind that, Sariel was demonstrating an unusual concern for Maou's health.

Lying back down on his futon, Maou took a deep breath. "…Sorry. Just shove it in the fridge wherever."

"All right."

Stepping into Room 201, Sariel swiftly began moving the contents of his plastic bag to the refrigerator.

"This stuff all looks pretty bad for a sick man."

"Ugh, Libicocco, you know… He has a child's palate, and he eats *so* much…"

"Well, that ship's sailed, huh? Want me to make you some porridge or something?"

"…You're being nice to me. It's creepy."

"Oh, sure, say whatever you want. I'm not here 'cause I want to be, you know. Once this is over, you better get on hands and knees in front of Ms. Iwaki and Ms. Kisaki, then start polishing their shoes with the back of your head. If it were anyone besides them asking me for this, I'd laugh in their face."

That order had, perhaps, a bit of Sariel's own tastes mixed into it.

"…Yeah, I'd feel terrible if I didn't do that much, at least."

Maou seemed oddly eager to accept that. It puzzled Sariel, who decided to just stay in the kitchen instead of listening to him ramble.

"So what's up?" he asked, chopping up some vegetables. "They only told me you had a health emergency, but what happened? It sounds like your little scheme was going well and you just had the final step left—the last battle, right? And *now* look what happened. Did you catch a cold from someone?"

"...Ahh..."

The bleary Maou groaned a little.

"...I got kissed."

"...Huh?"

"...By Chi... She said she loved me, and she kissed me... And then...the demonic force...in my body..."

Maou's voice was soft, almost lost in the noise of the city, but Sariel heard it loud and clear. It made him take the knife he was using to chop up chives and green onions, out of the benevolence of his heart, and go straight into archangel mode, pointing it at the King of All Demons.

"Devil King...are you trying to start a fight with me? With this bragging? Huh?"

The voice was shrill, but Maou just kept going in his soft warble.

"...Hey, Sariel?"

"What? Because I'm about to 'accidentally' put daffodil stems into your porridge instead of chives..."

"What's it mean to be loved by someone?"

"...Huh?"

The sudden question made the archangel cancel his Devil King poisoning project.

"I mean...logically, I get it. I do... I love Alas Ramus as family, and she loves me as her father, so... But, I..."

The archangel looked on, flummoxed.

"I don't know what love is when it's on the same eye level as me."

"...Huhh?"

Listening to the delirious ravings from the weakened Maou made him arch an eyebrow straight up, knife still in hand...

- To be continued -

THE AUTHOR, THE AFTERWORD, AND YOU!

From here on in, I'd like to ask a few questions.

When filling out your medical history at the dentist or health clinic, I think a lot of people have been asked how often they brush their teeth—but how often a day do you brush yours?

For anyone past grade-school age, unless you're so sick that you can't get out of bed, I imagine it's at least once a day. But while some people say they brush after every meal, others keep it to morning and night, since they can't do it at work or school. A lot of people probably do it just once before bedtime. But no matter what your habits, the people who brush after every meal probably can't believe those who keep it to every evening, and those who stick to once a day might think "Surely you don't need to do it after *every* meal, do you?"

Brushing your teeth, of course, is a part of dental hygiene, a habit that can pretty heavily affect how people judge you in public.

Now, let's zoom over to the next question. How often do you clean the bath, toilet, and sink in your home? Some people clean the bath every time they use it, while others probably don't feel it's worth it if they used only the shower. Some people clean the toilet every day, while others don't bother if it doesn't look too dirty. With the sink, sometimes it's an everyday thing; sometimes it's not seen as a biggie until scale starts to form.

Finally, what do you do with your dishes? Are you okay with having stacks of greasy dishes pile up in your sink? When you put them in the drying rack, do you try to align them all pretty, or do you just toss them in willy-nilly? And when you move them back to your cabinet, do you give them one more wipe beforehand, just in case there's any moisture left on them?

I'll go this far, but there are so many cases to consider that it's just annoying to categorize them all. That, and these days, the debate might be more about whether to just put your stuff directly into the dishwasher after eating, or to give them a quick rinse first.

You might be wondering where I'm going with this, but all these questions have to do with washing. And dishwasher manufacturers may have instructions on how to use them correctly, but with a lot of people, their washing habits don't really have a basis in logic.

One's choices along these lines, unfortunately, can affect their relationships to a potentially lethal level—and oddly enough, no two people take the exact same approach with everything. Some people use a stiffer toothbrush, unsatisfied until they're bleeding from their gums, only not to care about their tub until there's hair all over the place. Someone who won't rest until every inch of the tub surface is wiped up and toweled off might let plates with streaks of chili sauce and rice kernels sit in the sink for days. A person might insist on only using water strained through a filter, only to have no problem using leftover bathwater to wash other stuff.

All these personal opinions connect directly to someone's "cleanliness"—it's not a matter of what's right or wrong, what's efficient or inefficient. But someone's approach to this is really a representation of the life they've cultivated up to now. So unless you're doing something obviously separated from reality, like not brush for a week or not clean the toilet for a year, there's no absolutely right answer in modern society, and if you declare *your* way to be right and push it on others, you're probably not going to find many friends.

That's why, in situations like these, you need to talk things out and compromise with each other. Instead of simply refusing any possibility besides your own habits, you need to observe, digest, compromise if you can be convinced to, and if that's not possible, ask your partner to understand and discuss why you've adopted your respective habits.

* * *

    In the environment I wrote this book in, I often had the strong notion that the secret to preserving your relationship when living together—whether you're family, lovers, or friends—is not to neglect this kind of thing. In this story, two people who adopted different habits from the day they were born come to live together—an important factor to the tale. This pair, which defaulted to bloodshed at first, is now attempting to talk out a solution, and as the writer, I strongly hope they won't go back to those bad old days.

    The final resolution is left to the future story, and there's not much of it left! See you in the next volume!

HAVE YOU BEEN TURNED ON TO LIGHT NOVELS YET?

IN STORES NOW!

SWORD ART ONLINE, VOL. 1-22
SWORD ART ONLINE PROGRESSIVE 1-6

The chart-topping light novel series that spawned the explosively popular anime and manga adaptations!

MANGA ADAPTATION AVAILABLE NOW!

SWORD ART ONLINE © Reki Kawahara ILLUSTRATION: abec
KADOKAWA CORPORATION ASCII MEDIA WORKS

ACCEL WORLD, VOL. 1-24

Prepare to accelerate with an action-packed cyber-thriller from the bestselling author of *Sword Art Online*.

MANGA ADAPTATION AVAILABLE NOW!

ACCEL WORLD © Reki Kawahara ILLUSTRATION: HIMA
KADOKAWA CORPORATION ASCII MEDIA WORKS

SPICE AND WOLF, VOL. 1-21

A disgruntled goddess joins a traveling merchant in this light novel series that inspired the *New York Times* bestselling manga.

MANGA ADAPTATION AVAILABLE NOW!

SPICE AND WOLF © Isuna Hasekura ILLUSTRATION: Jyuu Ayakura
KADOKAWA CORPORATION ASCII MEDIA WORKS

IT WRONG TO TRY TO PICK UP GIRLS IN A DUNGEON?, VOL. 1-16

A would-be hero turns damsel in distress in this hilarious send-up of sword-and-sorcery tropes.

MANGA ADAPTATION AVAILABLE NOW!

Is It Wrong to Try to Pick Up Girls in a Dungeon? © Fujino Omori / SB Creative Corp.

ANOTHER

The spine-chilling horror novel that took Japan by storm is now available in print for the first time in English—in a gorgeous hardcover edition.

MANGA ADAPTATION AVAILABLE NOW!

Another © Yukito Ayatsuji 2009/ KADOKAWA CORPORATION, Tokyo

CERTAIN MAGICAL INDEX, VOL. 1-22

Science and magic collide as Japan's most popular light novel franchise makes its English-language debut.

MANGA ADAPTATION AVAILABLE NOW!

A CERTAIN MAGICAL INDEX © Kazuma Kamachi
ILLUSTRATION: Kiyotaka Haimura
KADOKAWA CORPORATION ASCII MEDIA WORKS

VISIT YENPRESS.COM TO CHECK OUT ALL THE TITLES IN OUR NEW LIGHT NOVEL INITIATIVE AND...

GET YOUR YEN ON!

www.YenPress.com

Discover the other side of Magic High School—read the light novel!

The Irregular at Magic High School

VOLUMES 1-15 AVAILABLE NOW!

Explore the world from Tatsuya's perspective as he and Miyuki navigate the perils of First High and more! Read about adventures only hinted at in *The Honor Student at Magic High School*, and learn more about all your favorite characters. This is the original story that spawned a franchise!

www.yenpress.com

IN THIS FANTASY WORLD, EVERYTHING'S A GAME—AND THESE SIBLINGS PLAY TO WIN!

A genius but socially inept brother and sister duo is offered the chance to compete in a fantasy world where games decide everything. Sora and Shiro will take on the world and, while they're at it, create a harem of nonhuman companions!

No Game No Life © Yuu Kamiya 2012
KADOKAWA CORPORATION

No Game No Life, Please! © Kazuya Yuizaki 2016 © Yuu Kamiya 2016
KADOKAWA CORPORATION

LIGHT NOVELS 1–9 AVAILABLE NOW

LIKE THE NOVELS?

Check out the spin-off manga for even more out-of-control adventures with the Werebeast girl, Izuna!

Follow us on

Yen Press

www.yenpress.com

Read the light novel that inspired the hit anime series!

Re:ZeRo
-Starting Life in Another World-

Also be sure to check out the manga series!
AVAILABLE NOW!

www.YenPress.com

Re:Zero Kara Hajimeru Isekai Seikatsu
© Tappei Nagatsuki, Daichi Matsuse / KADOKAWA CORPORATION
© Tappei Nagatsuki Illustration: Shinichirou Otsuka / KADOKAWA CORPORATION